HOT SEAL, RED WINE

SEALS IN PARADISE

BECCA JAMESON

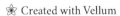 Created with Vellum

ACKNOWLEDGMENTS

Thanks to all the authors who participated in the SEALs in Paradise series! What an amazing group!

Hot SEAL, Salty Dog by Elle James

Hot SEAL, S*x on the Beach by Delilah Devlin

Hot SEAL, Dirty Martini by Cat Johnson

Hot SEAL, Bourbon Neat by Parker Kincade

Hot SEAL, Cold Beer by Cynthia D'Alba

Hot SEAL, Rusty Nail by Teresa Reasor

Hot SEAL, Black Coffee by Cynthia D'Alba

Hot SEAL, Single Malt by Kris Michaels

"Time and time again, Ms. Jameson infuses her talent for creating pleasurable and entertaining love stories with wonderful characters, a depth of passion, and the joy at discovering your soul mate that is beautiful and thoroughly sexy."

— SHANNON, THE ROMANCE STUDIO

"Becca Jameson can write sex, hot, steamy, make-you-cold-shower-twice sex. She also can write emotion."

— FELICITY NICHOLS, MAD IN
WONDERLAND REVIEWS

"I always love reading Becca Jameson's bedroom scenes and how she makes her heroes fall so completely in love with the female leads in her stories."

— RONI, ROMANCE BOOK SCENE

"Becca has the ability to create the different worlds, draw you into them, and keep you wanting more with her writing ability. The way she writes the different characters, you can't help but to feel for their emotions. When they are scared and upset, you are as well."

PROLOGUE

"Karla, I just don't see how I can pull it off. I'm so busy at work right now. A vacation is not in the cards." Ellie shuffled through the papers on her desk while she spoke to her best friend from high school, the phone on speaker and propped against a binder.

"Ellie, I haven't seen you in five years. You didn't even come home for our ten-year reunion. Pleeaase. Come. Join me. A girls' trip. I need this too. A cruise is perfect. We can drink all we want, eat until we're stuffed, catch up. It'll be fun."

Ellie sighed, leaned back in her chair, closed her eyes, and rubbed her temples. She had a headache. What else was new?

"Don't hesitate. Just say yes. It's seven days. You can fly into Houston, take a shuttle to Galveston, and meet me at the ship."

"Even if I did have an entire week available to me, I

couldn't possibly go on vacation someplace where I don't have easy access to internet." Even though she talked to Karla at least once a week, it was true she hadn't seen her in a very long time. She hadn't been back to the Houston area for years.

Karla groaned. "That's the entire point. You need to unwind. Stay off the internet. Disconnect. Relax. Flirt with men. Have a fling."

It was Ellie's turn to groan. "I don't do flings, and I suck at flirting."

"You live in New York City, Ellie. You don't even date. If I was living the high life you're living, I'd be out every other night with another man," Karla joked.

Ellie shook her head, even though her friend couldn't see her. "That's shit, and you know it. First of all, you would never leave League City. Second of all, you've been with Layton since we were like, fifteen. I know you would never even glance at another man."

Karla giggled. "Hey, I can pretend. In my head."

"Yeah, don't tell Layton that." Ellie smiled. She'd known both of them for most of her life. In high school, their posse—which included Ellie's boyfriend, Noah— had been inseparable. Noah and Layton had been pals since grade school too. They were both on the football team and hung out together every chance they got.

Ellie hadn't seen Karla and Layton for five years, the summer she went to their wedding.

She hadn't seen Noah since the day they graduated from high school. The memory still stung as a lump formed in her throat. Noah hadn't been able to get leave from the navy for the wedding.

"So, how about it?" Karla asked. "Please?"

Ellie frowned. "Why is Layton letting you go on a cruise without him?"

"He's too busy to take a week off this summer."

"So am I," Ellie returned.

Karla sighed heavily. "Layton takes off at least three weeks a year. We used his vacation to go to the mountains over Christmas. *You* haven't taken a single day off in years."

It was true. Ellie was burnt out. She hadn't come up for air in a very long time. It was easier for her. Kept her mind occupied. She'd been working on Wall Street for almost ten years. It was stressful. She loved it.

Didn't she?

Karla was an elementary school teacher. She had summers off. Every year she begged Ellie to come visit.

Ellie took a deep breath and accepted the invitation on a whim before she could change her mind. "Okay. I'll go. On one condition."

Karla squealed. "Anything."

"You plan the trip. I pay for the room. I'll give you my credit card."

Karla groaned. "I don't want you to do that."

"That's my condition. Take it or leave it." Ellie had made a lot of money in the last decade. She spent it on absolutely nothing. She had invested well and could afford any vacation in the world. She knew the same wasn't true of Karla working as a teacher with a husband who was a cop.

"Okay, but I'm paying for the excursions, then."

"Yeah, we'll see about that."

3

"I cannot *wait* to see you. This is going to be epic." The excitement in Karla's voice was worth it.

Ellie smiled. "Epic," she repeated.

"We're totally going to find you a man."

"We are so totally *not* going to find me a man," Ellie returned. She was perfectly fine without one. She was resigned to living a life filled with work.

The only man for her had been Noah Seager, and she'd let him go a long time ago. She could blame no one but herself. She would bear that cross for the rest of her life. She deserved it. But she'd given up the idea of replacing him years ago. No one measured up.

Perhaps it was cheesy and ridiculous, holding on to the memory of her one and only boyfriend from fourteen years ago, but she could still picture the way he looked into her eyes. The way he held her close. She'd given her virginity to him. She'd given her heart to him. And then she'd ruined everything, fled town, and left him.

Karla knew Ellie well, but even Karla didn't know the details of Ellie's breakup with Noah. However, Karla was more than aware of her best friend's pining. There was no doubt Karla's intention was to get Ellie to move on with her life.

It wouldn't happen, but the cruise would be wonderful anyway. And reconnecting with Karla in person would be awesome.

As if Karla read her thoughts, she said in a soft voice, "There are other men out there, Ellie. You just have to open your heart."

"Yeah, my heart is closed for business, Karla. And I'm okay with it."

Karla sighed. "We'll see."

CHAPTER 1

Six weeks later…

Ellie was late. So very late. The flight had been delayed, and she'd almost missed the last shuttle to the cruise ship. She had texted Karla several times to let her know she was late, but she hadn't had a chance to check her phone in the past hour since she'd gotten to the ship.

She was one of the last passengers to board before they closed the door. Frazzled and tired and relieved at the same time, she rushed through the ship toward the lido deck where Karla had said to meet her at the bar.

Ellie didn't bother heading for their room first. Her luggage would be delivered to the room, which left Ellie with nothing but her travel bag where she'd stuffed her purse. She needed a drink. She needed sun. She needed to take a deep breath and start relaxing.

The ship was bustling with activity as she made her

way through the throng of people wandering around, familiarizing themselves with the amenities. Her phone was buried somewhere in her bag, but she figured she would easily find Karla at the bar and let the fun begin.

When she stepped out into the sunshine, she immediately relaxed, letting her shoulders drop. Hopefully, after a few drinks, she would loosen up enough to wrap her mind around everything that had happened to upend her world in the last three days.

She still couldn't believe the decisions she'd made, and she couldn't wait to see the look on Karla's face when she told her.

She hitched her floral bag high onto her shoulder, smoothed her hands down her sundress, and closed her eyes for a moment. The thin dress had seemed ridiculous as she left her apartment that morning. She was used to wearing business suits every day to work. Professional pencil skirts and matching jackets. Blouses. Pumps.

Not this week. She'd gone shopping over the weekend and bought seven outfits. Summer clothes fitting for a cruise. Two new bikinis, even though she couldn't remember the last time she'd worn a two-piece. Sandals. Flowy skirts. Tank tops. Shorts. She'd probably gone overboard, but as long as she was taking her first real vacation in five years, she wanted to make the most of it.

The pale pink sundress she'd worn to board the ship made her feel younger than normal. It was a bit short, but she intended to be carefree this week. The spaghetti straps would have left her freezing on the plane, but she'd brought a light white sweater which was now stuffed in her bag.

A glance down at the bodice made her smile again. She liked the look. Maybe she could reinvent herself. Become a new woman. Her breasts looked amazing under the fitted cotton that dipped low enough to show more cleavage than she was used to.

Maybe she would lighten up and let Karla help her find a man. It couldn't hurt to at least have a vacation fling. Right? Who was she kidding? She'd never had a fling in her life.

With another deep breath, she forged ahead once more.

The bar was easy to find. It was also crowded. Several people were already lounging in the pool. Laughter and squeals of delight filled her ears. The grill was open. The scent of burgers and hotdogs hit her from the right. She couldn't remember the last time she'd had junk food, but she intended to indulge in it for seven days. Every day. Maybe even in the middle of the night.

She giggled out loud as she squinted into the sun and worked her way through the crowd.

Karla's bright red hair would stand out. She had the most gorgeous curls that framed her round face. Ellie had always been envious of her friend's hair. Ellie's own brown locks hung in long waves down her back. She'd hardly changed it since high school, and she hadn't had a chance to get it cut before she headed out of town.

When she finally reached the bar, she leaned against

it with both hands, trying not to let her bag bang into anyone. She scanned the entire area. No red hair.

The bartender caught her eye and leaned toward her to be heard over the crowd. He smiled. "Hi. Welcome aboard. What can I start you off with?" He pointed at a red-and-yellow swirly frozen drink behind him and told her it was the special of the day. She had no idea what he called it, but she nodded.

As he turned back around to fill the blender with rum and whatever else was going to start this trip off perfectly, she scanned the area again. Still no Karla. Perhaps she'd given up and headed for the room. She was probably in a panic.

Ellie realized she needed to find her phone and check her messages. As she tipped her head down to dig around in her bag, she heard her name and froze. "Ellie?" The voice was familiar. So familiar she would never forget it if she lived two hundred years. But it wasn't Karla's.

She slowly lifted her gaze to find her ears had not deceived her.

Noah Seager. In the flesh. He had closed the distance and was now leaning against the bar two inches from her. She could feel his breath as she tipped her head back to meet his gaze.

She swallowed, unable to speak.

Holy shit.

He looked so damn good. Taller. Broader. Tan. His hair was still the same deep brown, but it was cut shorter than it had been in high school. There were a few new lines around his eyes, which were currently narrowed in surprise. One corner of his mouth was lifted in a half-smile. The left corner. Same as she remembered.

He looked carefree in a white, button-up, short-sleeved shirt with several buttons undone, exposing his fantastic chest. He also wore khaki pants and loafers. His clothes all looked new as if he'd done the same as her and shopped recently for a new wardrobe.

"I can't believe it," he said. "Is it really you?"

She nodded slowly, though she wasn't certain it *was* her. Or him for that matter. It seemed surreal. What were the chances he would be on the same cruise as her? "Noah…" She let his name slide from her lips like an ocean wave.

"Ma'am?" The bartender interrupted her stunned shock, but she couldn't bring herself to glance away from Noah. Standing so close she could feel his warmth.

He apparently had more brain cells than her, however, because he took the drink from the bartender and signed a slip of paper.

She jerked her attention to the receipt when she realized what he was doing. "You don't have to do that."

He handed her the drink, frowning. "It's a drink. I think I can manage to buy you a drink."

She nodded, taking the cold glass from his hand. Their fingers brushed against each other, and she nearly swallowed her tongue. Her legs felt weak. She was afraid she would drop the drink, so she set it on the bar.

"Why don't you sit?" He pointed at the stool she was leaning against as he eased onto the one next to hers.

She let her bag slide down her arm to land on the

floor at her feet and somehow managed to jump up onto the seat. Her skirt was too short and didn't get tucked under her butt very well, but she simply didn't care.

Noah. Her Noah. The man she'd dreamed of for fourteen years. The man she'd only known as a teenager who had grown into someone ten times more handsome than she remembered. She could not believe this was happening.

His gaze roamed up and down her body, making her face heat. Suddenly it seemed much hotter than it had a moment ago. He slowly shook his head. "You look amazing."

"Thanks. You do too." How she managed to utter a word was a mystery. Her gaze was drawn to his full lips as he spoke, reminding her what they had felt like against hers. Against her neck. Her breasts. Her thighs. It had been so damn long...

"What are you up to these days?" he asked as he set his elbow on the bar.

He sat so close to her. Unbearably close. She wished she could reach up and touch him, remind herself what his skin felt like. The strength. The smooth texture.

"Ellie?"

Shit. He'd asked her a question. She nodded. "I live in New York."

He nodded. "Right. Layton told me that. You work on Wall Street, right?"

"Yes." She couldn't find the vocabulary to elaborate. "You?"

"I just finished my second tour with the SEALs."

She nodded. *Good job, Ellie. Way to hold a conversation.*

He chuckled. "I don't remember you being so quiet."

She forced a smile. "I guess I'm just shocked. You're here. On the same cruise as me. What are the chances?"

He frowned and glanced around, his eyes slowly narrowing. "Wait. Who are you with?"

"Karla. Girls' trip. We haven't seen each other in years."

He tipped his head back and groaned. "I should have known."

"What?" She sat up straighter, her spine stiffening at his tone.

He met her gaze once more, his expression serious. "I'm with Layton. Guys' week."

Her mouth fell open, her eyes nearly popping out of her head. "No."

He nodded. "Yes."

She looked around. "Where is he?" She would personally kill Layton and then Karla too.

"Haven't found him yet." He swiped a hand over his face. "Why the hell would they do this?"

"I can't imagine." Except she could. She could totally imagine. Karla had bugged Ellie about her breakup with Noah for years. Fourteen of them. Always prying for answers. Never getting anything out of Ellie.

"Do you think they have some wild idea they can get us back together by arranging a friends' cruise?"

"It would seem that way." She bit the corner of her lower lip hard. She was absolutely going to kill Karla. The moment she turned up.

Noah slid off the stool, running his free hand down his face. He didn't meet her gaze.

A renewed flush rushed over her cheeks and down her chest at his discomfort. She felt it too, but seeing him clearly wishing he could fall into the ocean put her on edge.

He finally glanced at her. "Look, I'm so sorry about this. I can't imagine why Layton would set us up like this. It's crazy. Water under the bridge. It's been fourteen years. I promise I knew nothing about this. I never would have agreed to come on this cruise if he'd told me."

Ellie nearly choked. He didn't have to be a dick about it.

Although, to be fair, he had every right to be a dick about it. In fact, she was surprised by how cordial he'd been up to that moment. Smiling and seeming genuinely happy to see her.

He tapped the bar with his fingers. "I'm going to go find Layton and toss him overboard. Don't worry about me. It's a big ship. We don't have to see each other. There's plenty to do." With those sharp parting words, he turned around and walked away.

Ellie stared at his back for long moments until she could no longer see him in the crowd. She couldn't move or breathe. It felt like she was swaying back and forth. And perhaps she was. She was on a ship after all. It was still docked, however.

Docked…

She jerked her gaze up, wondering if she could still get off the boat. At that very moment two loud blasts of the ship's horn sounded, signaling they were moving away from the dock.

Dammit.

Several announcements were made. She understood very few words. Her ears were ringing. She turned back to the bar and picked up the drink. It had melted enough to suck about half of it down in one swallow. She needed the alcohol.

She glanced around again, looking for red curls and finding nothing of the sort. Undoubtedly, Karla and Layton had conspired to get both Noah and Ellie to run into each other at the bar right off the bat, so they could start forging the imaginary relationship that would never happen. It *could* never happen.

What Karla and Layton didn't know was why Ellie had walked away from Noah to begin with. She'd never told a living soul. Not even Noah.

The damage had been thorough. There would never be any way to patch things up in forty years, let alone fourteen. Their friends were sadly mistaken if they thought they could arrange some sort of reconciliation.

Sure, maybe Noah had found a way to pretend to be polite and cordial for a few moments after running into her unexpectedly. But there was no way he would continue to do so for seven days. It wasn't like they could play nice, go to dinner together, plan the same excursions, hang out at the pool.

This vacation had taken a serious dive into murky waters.

Ellie wasn't ready to face Karla yet. She needed more time to gather her thoughts. Her friendship with Karla had lasted over two decades. The last thing Ellie wanted to do was cause irrevocable damage to their relationship while she was still fuming at her friend's horrible plan.

Setting two people up was always a gamble. Setting two people up without their knowledge would be outside the bounds of normal friendship. Setting two people up to spend a week on a cruise ship without checking with them first was unforgivable.

It wasn't really Karla's fault for thinking she might be able to get her high school friends to rekindle their relationship. She didn't have all the facts. All she knew was what Ellie had told her over the years. That information had been spotty, but Ellie had never suggested she was over Noah in any way. Because she was not. She never would be.

She sucked down the rest of her drink, noticing the deck was starting to clear.

"Ma'am?"

She glanced at the bartender.

"You need to report to your muster station."

She nodded and slid off her stool, hoping her legs could carry her to the designated spot. She wished she'd had time to drop her carry-on bag in her room, but apparently not. She would have to drag it with her to listen to the speech about escape routes, passenger safety, and lifeboats.

As soon as the drill was over, she would find her room and then hunt Karla down. By then, she hopefully would have calmed down enough to keep from shouting.

She had no idea how she was going to live through seven days on the same ship as Noah. The once massive ship she'd seen from the pier just an hour ago suddenly seemed ten times smaller. It was shrinking by the minute.

CHAPTER 2

Noah tossed his cell phone on the bed and paced the small room. This could not be happening.

He'd spent the last hour trying unsuccessfully to get ahold of Layton. He'd even called Karla and gotten nothing but her voicemail. Where the hell were those two?

He ran a hand over his head and wandered toward the balcony. This was going to be the most challenging week of his life, but at least the room was amazing and the view off the balcony spectacular. If he had to spend the entire time alone in the room, he would manage.

He had assumed he and Layton would be sharing the room, and had been surprised to find it had only one king-sized bed. Layton and he had been close friends since second grade, but no way would Layton have booked a room with only one bed.

Noah hadn't been able to help with the arrangements at all. He'd been stuck overseas until a week ago and then taking care of paperwork and debriefing for several days as he prepared to leave the SEALs.

The few times he spoke with Layton, his friend had assured him everything was a go and not to worry. All he had to do was show up and relax.

Noah hadn't been on vacation in years. He'd been to a lot of countries with his SEAL team, but not one moment of that time could have been considered leisure.

Unable to breathe, he opened the sliding door to the balcony and stepped out into the humid Galveston air. He grabbed the railing with both hands and stared at the shoreline as they moved farther and farther from land.

He was officially trapped on a boat with the woman he'd loved more than anything in the world fourteen years ago. The woman who'd broken his heart and left him just days before he reported to the navy.

Why the fuck did she have to look so damn good? She had been gorgeous at eighteen. She was a drop-dead knockout today. All that thick, wavy hair that hung longer than he'd ever seen her wear it. Those sexy green eyes that seemed to pierce into his soul.

Those pink lips. Damn those lips. And when she bit the lower one… "Shit." He'd almost reached out to pluck it from between her teeth before he caught himself and remembered not only was she not his to touch anymore, but he was supposed to be pissed with her.

She was more filled out than she had been in high

school, which was also in her favor. Her hips were slightly wider. Her breasts were fuller. That dress…

He squeezed his eyes closed, wishing he'd never seen her again while knowing at the same time it would take him twice as many years to forget those few minutes on the lido deck with her. Every single move she made had gotten to him. The way she shifted on the stool. The way her skirt had ridden up her thighs when she sat. The way her hands shook when she realized they'd been set up.

"Shit," he repeated.

A noise behind him had him spinning around, expecting to find the cabin steward delivering his luggage.

Instead, his breath stopped in his lungs.

There she was.

Ellington Gorman.

His first love.

In his cabin.

Why?

He shoved off the railing and stepped back into the room.

Her eyes were bugged out again, and she dropped her bag to the floor. "Why are you in my room?" she asked.

"I was about to ask you the same thing."

She glanced around. "This is my room," she repeated as if echoing her words would make them more real.

"Apparently it's my room too." Yes, he was going to throw Layton overboard. Karla too. If he found them fast enough, maybe they could swim to shore without drowning. What were they thinking?

"We can't share a room," she stated.

"Obviously," he agreed completely. Not a chance in hell. Perhaps he could take a few minutes to be nice to a girl he'd once dated in high school upon running into her for the first time in fourteen years, but this was asking too much. She fucking broke up with him. She literally broke his heart, though he'd never admit that out loud. He'd been a dude, for Christ's sake. He still was a dude.

She licked her lips. "We need to find our stupid friends."

"Agreed. I haven't had any luck. They're both ignoring my calls and texts. I don't even know what room they're in. I assumed I was sharing this one with Layton." He pointed at the bed. "Though I was shocked to find only one bed." He shuddered. The idea of sleeping in that bed with Ellie was almost as distasteful as doing so with his friend.

She reached down, picked up her bag, set it on the bed, and began to dig around in it. "I haven't checked my phone for a while. I was late. Almost missed the final boarding. In my rush, I hurried straight for the bar where Karla told me to meet her."

He couldn't hold back his sarcasm when he said, "Imagine that. Layton also told me to meet him at the bar."

She found her phone, ignoring him, and touched the screen. "Dammit."

"What? Please tell me Karla at least left you a message."

She held it out, screen toward him. "Not a single word since I told her I was going to make it by the skin of my teeth a few hours ago."

"Fuck," he proclaimed a bit louder than he intended. What he wanted to do was grab something heavy and throw it across the room. But he'd never been a violent man in his civilian life before, and he wouldn't start now.

"Okay," Ellie started calmly. "So, we get another room. I'll go to the front desk and straighten this out. You keep trying to find our friends."

She turned around, but just as she reached for the doorknob, he spoke again. "How close are you and Karla?"

"She's my best friend. Why?" Ellie looked at him over her shoulder, her brows drawn together.

"Just wondering if you'd mind if I tossed their bodies over the side of the ship when I find them."

She gave him a slow smile, one like the million he'd received from her when they were teenagers. Conspiring. Cute. Sexier than he remembered. "Be my guest." And then she was gone.

He was still staring at the door when a soft knock sounded and it opened again. He expected Ellie, thinking she had something else to say or forgot something, but it was the cabin steward. "I have your luggage, sir," he stated.

Noah stared completely dumbfounded as the man

piled four suitcases into the room. Two of them were Noah's. He assumed the other two were Ellie's.

Insanity. Pure and total insanity.

He nodded at the steward and then picked up his phone to call Layton again.

No signal.

Great.

The phone was now essentially useless for the next seven days. Turning it off, he dropped it on the nightstand and glanced around the room. He'd never been on a cruise before, but he'd always been told how small the cabins were. People talked like they could barely move around. The only thing that fit in the room was the bed or beds. Just enough space between them to squeeze past.

This room was somewhat larger than he'd expected. It was also located at the back of the ship with a balcony and spectacular view. Who the hell had paid for the room? Noah certainly hadn't.

It seemed absurd that Layton and Karla would have sprung for this room in order to get Noah and Ellie back together, but maybe they had. Apparently he didn't know his friend at all. Perhaps the guy had won the lottery recently and didn't tell anyone. He didn't think, between the two of them, they made enough money to throw it around. In fact, he was fairly certain they were trying to start a family.

Noah could afford the room. Not that he'd made millions of dollars with the navy or later on the SEAL team, but he also hadn't had many expenses. So, he'd invested most of his salary every year, hoping for a nest egg to give him some wiggle room when he left the SEALs. That day was now.

As pissed as he was, he would find out how much Layton had paid for this room and give the man a check. He wondered how long Karla and Layton would remain incommunicado. Hell, he wondered if they knew what room they'd assigned to Ellie and Noah. Perhaps theirs was close by. Could even be next door.

He shoved off the bed and stepped back onto the balcony to lean around the right and then the left, trying to see any sign of his friends.

Nothing.

If they were in one of the rooms next door, they were hiding. Which was probably good because he figured he had the upper body strength to reach around the wall dividing the rooms, grab another human by the shirt, and drop whoever it was into the water.

He could not spend time with Ellie. Not any time. Not one minute. Not a chance in hell. He sure as shit wasn't sharing a room with her. As pissed as he was with Layton, he had an idea. Those two might have thought to spend a cozy vacation having sex and enjoying each other, but they were so very wrong. The moment he found them, he would make them separate. Karla could move in with Ellie. Noah would bunk with Layton. Even if there was only one damn bed.

Yes. If Ellie was unable to get another room, his plan would work.

He stepped back inside just as another knock sounded at the door. Expecting to find Ellie once again, he hurried over to open it. At least she was polite enough to knock and not just walk in. Or better yet, maybe she didn't have a key to his room anymore.

Again, the person at the door was not Ellie. It was a ship employee in a navy polo shirt with the ship's logo in the corner. She smiled brightly and held out a large basket filled with chocolates, wine, glasses, and fruit. "Delivery for Ellington Gorman and Noah Seager," she declared, far too cheerily.

Noah reminded himself nothing was this woman's fault. He took the basket from her, forced a nod of acknowledgment, and turned back to the room as the door slid shut behind him.

He set it on the desk space and dug around for a card. His fingers were shaking for reasons he could not explain as he opened the card and read it. He read it again. And again. "Son of a bitch," he muttered just as the door to the room opened again.

Ellie stepped inside, deflated, her face speaking for her. She dropped her bag on the floor and met his gaze. "Every room on this ship is occupied."

"Oh, I can top that," he informed her.

She slowly shook her head. "Please tell me you've found Karla and Layton."

"Yep. I found them all right." He pointed to the basket. "They had this delivered." He held out the card and delivered the final blow. "They aren't on this ship. They never were."

Legs unwilling to hold him up any longer, he lowered to the edge of the bed.

The card fluttered to the floor because Ellie hadn't

taken it from him. She stood staring at him without moving. Like a wax figure. She wasn't even blinking.

After a few seconds, her face turned white, and he thought she might faint.

If he could have moved fast enough, he would have reached out to catch her before she hit the floor, but he was drained of all energy.

Luckily, she didn't pass out. She simply gave up the fight to remain upright, let her knees bend, and lowered herself to the floor. Her knees hit first, and then she dropped to her butt and leaned against the end of the bed, head in her hands.

They remained that way in total silence for a long time. He had no idea how long. He was busy processing. Thinking. His thoughts were a jumbled mess, however. Nothing made sense.

He only knew one thing—he couldn't do this. He couldn't share a room with Ellie. Not even one night. Not even one more minute.

A soft noise caught his attention, and he lifted his head. A moment later, he knew what he was hearing. She was crying.

Shit.

He could endure a lot of things, but not Ellie's tears. Not even the tears she'd shed while she was breaking up with him. Even then, he'd reached out to her. Of course, he'd been hoping to change her mind, but still.

Unable to stop himself, mainly because he wasn't an asshole, he slid off the bed, came to her side, dropped down next to her, and pulled her into his arms.

She tucked her head against his chest, sobbing

harder as he threaded his fingers into her soft, thick hair.

He wanted to tell her everything would be okay, but he knew that wasn't true. Nothing would ever be okay again. It wasn't possible. Not after touching her like this. Holding her. Feeling her against him. She fisted his shirt in her hand and leaned closer.

Finally, after a long time, she lifted her face and met his gaze. Streaks of tears were on her cheeks. Her eyes were bloodshot. Her mascara was smudged. Her lips were dry. She licked them and said the last thing he expected. "I'm so sorry. I never meant to hurt you."

CHAPTER 3

Ellie's world was a blur. Emotional overload made her heavy and tired. She was aware of leaning into Noah, and then he picked her up and set her on the bed. He tugged the covers down, slid her sandals off, and tucked her in.

She let her eyes close, ducked her face into the pillow, and cried again. She didn't even know why she was crying. She didn't deserve to feel this pain and sadness. She'd hurt him. Terribly. It didn't matter what her reasons were. She could fully understand why he would hate her for the rest of his life. He owned that. He had every right to hate her. And here she was, in his room, lying on his bed, on his pillow, in his space, breathing his air.

As if she had a right to any of it.

She did not.

She must have dozed because when she opened her eyes the next time, it was dark outside. The sliding door was still open, and she could see Noah sitting on the balcony. His bare feet were propped on the glass wall. He had a large dark bottle in his hand. Wine? Probably from the basket.

She sat up, still feeling groggy, and slid off of the bed. On silent feet, she padded to the balcony and then dropped onto the empty chair next to his.

He didn't fully acknowledge her except to glance her way and nod slightly before returning his gaze to the sea.

For several minutes, she enjoyed the feel of the warm breeze that tossed her hair in every direction. She didn't bother to try to tame it. Instead, she pulled her feet up onto the chair in a totally unladylike manner, drawing her knees to her chest and propping her chin on her skirt. She was covered. Sort of. Enough.

She had no idea what to say or do next, so she went with her first thought. "What are you drinking?"

He lifted the bottle, glanced at the label, and responded, "Merlot."

She shuddered. *Gross.*

He glanced at her. "I'm not always this uncouth, but I didn't want to wake you looking around for a glass."

She shrugged. "I don't care what vessel you use to drink it. It's the contents that I find unappealing." She hoped he heard at least a hint of teasing in her voice.

"Hey, now. Don't make fun of my wine. I get that enough from my SEAL team. It's sophisticated. What do you like to drink? Please don't tell me it's always frozen and colorful like that shit you had on the lido deck."

She smiled. "No. Never. No idea what that was. I

couldn't hear what the bartender said. I just nodded. It was the drink of the day or something. My preference is gin and tonic."

He made a face. "Now *that's* gross. Gin gives me a hangover."

They went back to silence for a few moments, and then her stomach growled.

He spoke again. "I thought about waking you for dinner, but you looked so…"

"Yeah. I've been working too many hours for too many years. I can't tell you when I've had a nap like that. Nor can I tell you when I've been as stressed as I was this afternoon." Her voice faded. She'd nearly had a meltdown.

"The main dining room is still open if you want to go eat a sit-down meal. Or we could hit one of the dozen choices on the lido deck." He hesitated, and then turned to face her fully. "Or, if I'm being presumptuous and you'd rather I left you alone so you can enjoy your vacation, you can do whatever you want."

She swallowed the lump in her throat. "No. I mean, you're fine. We should probably clear the air, so we don't spend the week walking on eggshells."

"I don't think I feel like rehashing the past," he stated in a harsh tone. "But I'm not opposed making a plan we can both agree on for the week. I haven't had a vacation in forever, so I don't intend to let this ruin my fun. I'm sure you can agree with me on that."

"Yes." Her voice was soft. Mousy. Almost a squeak. She could hardly breathe, listening to him. For one thing, his voice was deeper and sexier than it used to be, and she felt her insides wanting to squirm. For another thing, he was pissed, and he didn't intend to let her forget it. Even if he was going to be cordial.

"So, let's set some boundaries and make a plan," he proposed.

"Okay." More mousy. More squeaky. *Dammit*.

He twisted his neck around to face the room. "The bed is big. We have no other options. Surely we can share it without too much difficulty."

She nodded. Her mind went to places it should not. Visions of his naked chest, his broad shoulders, his thighs… It had been so long since she'd touched him. Did he really think they could sleep next to each other without a problem? The thought of climbing between those sheets so close to him made her nearly hyperventilate.

And what was she going to wear? She had expected to be sleeping with Karla, so she hadn't brought sexy lingerie or anything. But she also hadn't brought nun's attire. It was going to be warm all week. She had tiny tank tops and flimsy shorts and a few cute nighties.

"You're going to have to help me out here, Ellie. I'm not a mind reader."

She flinched and lowered one foot to the floor. "Sorry. I'm not sure what to say. Whatever you want to do is fine." *After all, I'm the one who broke up with you. I should get no say in what happens from here.*

He narrowed his gaze. "Not good enough."

"Why not?" She sat up straighter. His look was so intense, it pierced her. Yeah, he was pissed. Her bottom lip quivered, and she pulled it in between her teeth. She had caused him so much pain, and he had not forgiven her. Why should he?

He groaned and tipped his head back. "Don't do that."

"Do what?" She had no idea what he was talking about.

He shoved off the chair, took a long drink from his bottle, and leaned over her. His hands landed on the arms of the chair, pinning her. His face was inches from hers. "Cry. Don't cry. I can't take it when you cry. It ruins my legitimate mad." He pushed off the chair and took two strides into the room.

For a moment, she sat there, stunned, watching his back, unable to do anything else. A tear escaped, and she swiped it away. She would not cry in front of him. She took a deep breath and followed him into the small room. Leaning against the open sliding door, she found her voice. "I'm sorry. I'll do my best. I'm emotional. I've had a rough… It doesn't matter. Just…" She sucked in air. "Just give me some time to pull myself together. A full night's rest will help."

He nodded, his back to her. "Fine." His suitcase was open, and he was fumbling around in it.

Her stomach made its emptiness known again. "I guess I should go find something to eat." She couldn't imagine going through the motions of chewing or swallowing, but she was hungry.

He nodded again. "Okay." He pulled out a shirt, tossed it on the bed, and unbuttoned the one he was wearing. Seconds later, his white summer shirt landed on the bed, and he picked up the stylish maroon polo and pulled it over his head.

She watched every second, holding her breath. He was so gorgeous. A few tattoos graced his back that hadn't been there when they were teenagers, but other than that, he was exactly as she remembered, but better.

Finally, he faced her. "I don't feel like getting dressed up, so I'm going to hit the lido deck. You want to come with me or go separate ways?"

"I'll go with you." Her voice was so soft. It was all she could manage.

"Okay. Let's go then." He leaned down and grabbed her sandals, handed them to her, and waited for her to take them.

She slid them on her feet. Nothing had been done in their room yet. No unpacking. Nothing. The suitcases sat where the cabin steward had left them. Except for the one Noah had opened.

"I should probably fix my makeup and comb my hair," she suggested.

He waved a hand toward the small bathroom.

She eased past him, unable to do so without touching him. After grabbing her makeup bag from her carry-on, she entered the restroom and shut the door. And then she breathed.

Holy mother of God. What the absolute hell had Karla and Layton been thinking? This was the most ridiculous arrangement they could have concocted.

Her hands were shaking as she cleaned off her mascara and reapplied it. She brushed her teeth, combed through her thick hair, and applied lip gloss. It was going to have to be enough. Noah was waiting for her.

When she opened the door, she found him leaning casually against the desk, ankles crossed, gaze on her as if he'd been watching for her to return. His expression was serious. Sad. So many emotions played across his face.

"I'm ready," she declared, smoothing a hand down her wrinkled dress. She didn't have the energy to change, nor did she have any idea what she would put on or where. They were really going to have to discuss this arrangement soon. It wasn't as if changing could occur in the bathroom. It was more like a two-foot closet. Even a person her size could barely turn around in there. If she set clothing down on any surface, it would get wet or fall on the floor.

He had his loafers back on, and he opened the door and let her pass under his arm. He even handed her a keycard, though she had no idea where he'd gotten it. She'd probably dropped it on the bed or floor when she returned earlier, arriving as if she'd come from a death march to the gallows.

She followed him down the hallway, slightly to his left. She couldn't remember where the lido deck was, but he managed to get them there easily.

Silently, they wandered through the entire floor, learning the options they would be selecting from for the next seven days as if by mutual agreement. When they got back where they'd started, he finally spoke. "I think I'm going to do the pasta bar. You?"

"That actually sounds good. I'll do the same." She

could choose something light and easy to eat. Her uncertainty about her ability to chew and swallow still lingered. Especially if she was going to share a table with Noah.

He nodded, and they headed toward the scent of red sauce and garlic. This floor of the ship appeared to be mostly comprised of food from end to end. Half of it was inside and half outside. It wasn't too crowded, but most people were probably in the dining room for their first perfect meal. She knew they had an assigned table at a specific time because it was on her keycard, but that didn't mean they had to make that choice every night. Or any night for that matter.

As if Noah read her mind, he turned toward her, handed her a plate from the stack next to the pasta bar, and said, "A cruise is all about the dining room. We should eat there most nights. But I think we're both a little off-kilter tonight. Let's grab some food, find a seat, and talk."

She agreed with another nod and followed him through the line, selecting pasta, red sauce, Alfredo sauce, Caesar salad, and a bread stick. Her plate was full, but she hoped she might find the energy to eat once she got started.

Noah turned back to her at the end of the line. "Inside or out?"

"Either is fine."

He cocked his head. "Is that going to be your standard answer all week?"

"Maybe…"

He sighed, grabbed his tray, and found them a table

out on the deck. "It's nice outside. Hopefully the weather will be like this the entire time."

"It should be. I looked at the report."

"Of course you did." She wasn't sure how to read his words, but a glance at his face showed that half-smile. He was teasing. And he knew her well, even fourteen years later.

After settling in his chair and opening his napkin, he spoke again, "I don't think we ever arrived at any event unprepared for the weather in high school. You always knew when it was going to rain or if we needed sunscreen or if it would be too cool for short sleeves. Nothing got by you."

He was right.

"I like to be prepared."

He dug into his plate of food and groaned immediately. "Delicious. It's not the main dining room, but it's still fantastic."

She took a tentative bite after him and agreed. The creamy Alfredo sauce melted in her mouth and urged her to continue. Before she knew it, her plate was clean. She lifted her gaze to find Noah leaning back in his chair, elbows on the arms, fingers threaded loosely across his lap. He was watching her. "I always loved how you enjoy your food."

She blushed and wiped her mouth. He said nothing else for a long time, but his gaze never left her. She could feel him soaking her in. Judging? Deciding what to do next?

Two small children raced past them, dripping from the pool, giggling. She watched them, a smile forming on her face.

"You still like kids," he pointed out.

She said nothing.

"You used to babysit them. You told me you wanted four." His gaze was still pinning her in place.

"I was young." She fidgeted, unable to stand his scrutiny. Was he going to reminisce like this all week, dissecting her? Because it would kill her. She remembered the plans they'd made as if it were yesterday. *He'd* been the one who wanted four kids. She was pretty sure he'd named them too. He'd had it all planned out. Every detail. Finish high school, join the navy, become a SEAL. The security from his job would launch them into the next phase—marriage and kids. A chill shook her body. If only life had been that simple.

"You were eighteen when you left me."

His choice of words made her flinch.

"An adult. You were always so vibrant and happy. Excited about the future. Excited about college. Excited about us…" His voice trailed off.

She fought back the tears that threatened again. "People change," she whispered.

"No, they don't."

She flinched.

He leaned forward, setting his elbows on the table. "They don't change. I've thought about it thousands of times. Something else changed. Something happened. You wouldn't tell me then. Will you tell me now?"

She shook her head slowly. "It's water under the bridge, Noah."

"It's more like a tsunami coming up over the ship

right now. Do you know how many times I've asked myself this question?"

She could imagine. She played with the corner of her napkin, staring at her empty plate. This week was going to be a disaster if he badgered her constantly over their breakup fourteen years ago.

He continued. "I've beaten myself to death trying to figure out if I did something or said something to make you turn away from me. I considered crawling back to you so many times over the years to beg your forgiveness for my unknown transgression."

She jerked. It shocked her to know he'd thought about her that often.

"I can see why Layton thought this would be a good idea. If you've spoken of me to Karla over the years the way I've talked about you with Layton, then no wonder they thought they should try to get us to reconnect. Ingenious really. Trapping us on a cruise ship in the same cubicle of a room for a week." He chuckled, but it wasn't with humor. His voice was slightly scary.

She wanted to shove away from the table, run from him, hide. Anywhere. But like he said, they were trapped for seven days on a cruise ship that no longer seemed as large as it had in the brochure.

"You have, haven't you? Spoken of me to Karla over the years, I mean."

She swallowed, but didn't answer him. It was a moot point. Of course she had.

"Interesting. I'm trying to wrap my head around this and figure out what to do next." He lifted one hand and rubbed his chin with his thumb. "I mean, we have so many options. I keep changing directions. To no avail. You don't seem willing to respond to any tactic I take.

"If I prod you, you'll retreat from me. If I don't, we'll be living a lie. I could push you away and leave you to yourself for a week. I've considered that option. We could agree not to speak to each other and come and go from the cabin at different times. Hell, one of us could sleep days and the other nights. Shifts."

She felt the blood draining from her face at his speech.

"Or I could take a different path, ignore our history, and charm the pants off you until you climb willingly into my side of the bed and take me into your sweet, sexy body."

She jerked her gaze up at his unexpected words, her eyes going wide as she met his smirk.

"At least I know you're listening."

There were no words. He was all over the place. She had no idea how to respond.

"I think something in the middle. I mean, we're stuck together for seven days. Physically, I'm as attracted to you as I was fourteen years ago." He shook his head rapidly. "No, that's not true. You're far more gorgeous than you were then. A woman. Not a teenager. You have curves you didn't have then. If I didn't know you and I was trolling around on this ship looking for someone to woo, I would still pick you over every other woman on the boat."

So very Noah. Always open and communicative. He'd never failed to display his emotions both on his face and in his words. It was one of the things she'd loved about him. He wasn't like other guys. He'd always made her feel special. He could charm her without effort. Apparently he still could.

She flushed and found her voice. "That feeling is, um, mutual." She hadn't changed either. Accepting a compliment from him had made her face heat fourteen years ago, and it still did now.

He smiled. "Good. One step in the right direction. Look at us agreeing on something. And now I know one thing you unintentionally divulged."

She tipped her head to one side. "What's that?"

"You didn't break up with me because you had fallen out of love with me. Of that I was always certain, except when I let doubt creep in."

She couldn't leave him with the impression she hadn't loved him. She couldn't lie to him about something that important. Her mouth opened and words flew out without filter. "I never stopped loving you."

He flinched. His face went hard. He looked like he might erupt and launch the table on its side, causing their dishes to go flying across the room. Instead, he looked away, took several deep breaths, and came back to center. "Jesus, Ellie. I want to shake some sense into of you. You ripped me to shreds. What did I do?"

"Let it go. Please, I beg you to let it go. Even if I told you what happened that spring, it wouldn't fix anything. It would only make things worse. You need to know that now. Asking me over and over will only put a wall up between us."

He nodded slowly.

Having found her voice, she took a breath and continued. "Noah, we're at an impasse. We can never get past this. It's impossible. You're the sort of person who would never be able to accept that you'll never know why I broke up with you, and I'm the sort of person who will take that information to the grave. So, you see, we can't fix it. We can't make things right between us. We—"

He interrupted, "Does Karla know?"

She shook her head.

He sighed. "So, that's why she optimistically thinks we can fix things."

"Yes. She has nagged me for years."

His voice was lower when he asked the next question. "Does *anyone* know?"

"No."

"What about me? Do *I* know?"

She groaned. This game had to end. "No. Noah, you don't. You didn't do anything. You didn't cause anything. Stop beating yourself up. I told you that then, and I'm still telling you that now. Let. It. Go."

He frowned.

"You've been wasting your time trying to figure out what path to take during this cruise. You need to accept that we will never be able to get back together because we have a fundamental difference of opinion over a topic you cannot fix. You have two options. Walk away from me or help me plan the vacation of a lifetime with kick-ass excursions and fine dining."

He stared at her. Thinking?

"I'll totally understand if you'd rather not waste your

41

vacation on a woman you can never have. It would be cruel to lead you to believe otherwise. It won't hurt my feelings if you want to set up a schedule to share the room so that we don't run into each other. You'll be free to canvas the ship, find someone with potential I don't have, and enjoy yourself." It stung to say those words. Badly. But leading him to believe he could ever have a future with her would not be fair.

The tables had turned because Noah blinked, totally out of words apparently.

She smiled. "On the flip side, I'd be willing to plot and plan seven amazing days with you as you suggested. We could relax, eat, drink, dance, eat some more, take excursions… I would never regret it. But you have to do so knowing we can't be together when this trip is over."

She leaned closer. "Noah, we can't be together because I'll never be able to answer the question you're never going to let go of." It hurt. It hurt so badly she wanted to scream at the cruelness of the universe. Instead, she breathed in and out, rapid breaths as if she'd been running.

She wasn't sure he was breathing at all. His eyes were wildly searching her face. Maybe he was trying to decide how serious she was. Finally, he tipped his head down and rubbed his temples with the thumb and middle finger of one hand. And then he rose from the table. "Can you make it back to the room okay? I think I'll wander around the deck a bit and consider your ultimatum."

She sighed. "I'm not sure I would call it an ultimatum."

"Really? What else would you call it?" His words were clipped. Angry. He shook himself and stepped back. "Sorry. I need to clear my head. I'll meet you back at the cabin." And then he walked away.

CHAPTER 4

Noah was out of his mind with confusion. Ellie had him tied in such tight knots, he didn't think they could be undone. He had needed to get as far away from her as possible before he grabbed her by the shoulders and forced her to open up to him.

It hadn't worked then, and it wouldn't work now. She was a stubborn woman.

Not that he'd ever grabbed her, nor would he ever. But he wanted to. He wanted her as badly today as he had fourteen years ago. They'd had plans together. A lifetime of plans. He squeezed his eyes closed as he remembered how they would sit up late talking about their futures. College for her. The navy and then the SEALs for him. Then they would get married, have kids, and live happily ever after.

It hadn't mattered that they wouldn't immediately get married because the promise was there; they'd known they were perfect for each other. Time wouldn't change that. It would only make them stronger.

Except something went horribly wrong with that plan. Or else he'd been duped and had been the only one on board all along.

No. He refused to believe that. She had loved him with every inch of her soul. He'd never doubted it. Not once. And if he studied her closely now, he would swear nothing had changed for her. She had a secret. A huge one. One she insisted she would never tell. One so big that he would bet his last dollar it hurt her to hold it because she knew as well as he did that she was his. For a lifetime.

She hadn't married. As far as Layton had conveyed, she didn't even date. Instead of following through on their original plans for her to get her teaching degree while he worked hard to reach his goal of one day becoming a Navy SEAL, she had taken a totally different path. She worked on Wall Street. Worked herself to the bone, according to their friends.

Did she do that so she didn't have to feel anything? Had she spent her life hiding from feelings she still had for him? It was possible he'd let his imagination get carried away thinking such things.

He made his way to the edge of the deck, grabbed the railing, and held on as if his life depended on it. He feared his knees would buckle as he considered Ellie's life. Her feelings. Her thoughts. Her love.

She wore her emotions on her sleeve. Her face betrayed her. Those deep green eyes gave away some of her secrets. Not the important ones. Just the ones that permitted him to see into her soul.

Fuck but she was obstinate. It would drive him crazy for his entire life if she never gave him answers. Closure. What did she mean when she said her leaving had nothing to do with him?

He'd never been more confused in all these years than he was now. Fourteen years ago, she'd convinced him she didn't want a long-distance relationship, that she thought they should go their separate ways and see other people, that it would be too hard to maintain what they had when they knew they would go for months without seeing each other for the next several years.

He'd been too stunned that night to stop her from leaving. She'd run him over like a bulldozer and left him shocked and frozen. And then she'd left town before dawn the next morning. Gone. Her parents knew nothing. Her sister didn't either. No one. Not even Karla.

Apparently she had returned home weeks later, but according to Layton, Ellie had never spoken to Karla about where she'd been or why she'd left. By the time she returned later that summer, Noah had already gone to basic training.

He'd been so hurt and angry and pissed; he'd wasted his last few days before joining the navy mentally telling her to fuck herself. But over the following months and years, he'd softened and begun to wonder what her motive was. Not him... Hmmm... That only caused him to add about ten billion more question to the list in his mind.

He truly lived in the most fucked-up world. A universe that insisted on keeping two people apart for a lifetime while only allowing one party to know why.

Goddammit he wanted her. As much today as he had in high school. He wasn't the same person he'd been back then. He'd dated. Many women. None more than a few times, but plenty of them. SEALs never had a problem finding a willing woman to spend an evening with.

He'd used other women to attempt to fill a hole in his chest. Not that he slept with all of them. He was discerning about who came to his bed. But he dated many. It had never worked. No one had ever been Ellie.

He cringed as he remembered telling Layton that, one time a few months ago. No wonder his friend had gone to such great lengths to arrange this. If neither he nor Karla had a clue why Ellie left Noah to begin with, they could easily believe the situation was fixable.

Noah shoved off the railing and strode along the deck to another spot, lifting his gaze to the sky. He pondered her options. They weren't much different from the ones he'd presented, but in a way they were. His were choices. Hers were ultimatums with no promise of a future.

It would kill him if he gave her his heart and she stomped on it and let him go at the end of their week together. Destroy him in a way he couldn't yet begin to imagine.

He tipped his head back farther and stared at the

sky. So bright. Promising. So many stars. The air was so clean and clear and filled with possibility.

He took several cleansing breaths and admitted to himself he was wandering aimlessly for no good reason. There had only ever been one option. He'd known as much as soon as he spotted her on the lido deck that afternoon, wearing that sexy sundress. He had to have her again. Which meant he had one choice—pursue her. Make her love him. Make her fall so hard for him that she had no choice but to change her mind. He had seven days to convince her she was his and force her to give up her stupid secret.

Challenge accepted.

He turned around and strode back across the deck toward the interior dining area and then hit the stairs. Ellington Gorman was in his cabin in his bed. What the hell was he doing outside? He had work to do.

No. There were no other options because Ellie was his one shot at happiness. If he didn't win her, there would be no replacement women.

And the craziest part of all? He knew the same was true for her. The stubborn woman thought she could go to her grave with her damn secret and her loneliness.

Fuck no.

Game on.

When he reached their cabin, he paused to bring himself under control. He needed to reach out to her in a way that would make her melt. She had always responded to his touch. He could do this.

He finally opened the door. The room was dark except for the stream of light coming from the moon.

The door to the balcony was open several inches, letting in the humid air and the sound of the waves and the ship's engine.

She was on the ocean side of the bed, facing the wall of glass, and she rolled to her back. "You can close the door if you want. It just felt so…"

"Claustrophobic?"

"Yeah."

"It's fine." He felt his way around the edge of the bed and entered the bathroom, still trying to figure out what to say to her. He brushed his teeth, used the toilet, washed his hands, and returned. When he got to the edge of the bed, he pulled his shirt over his head, dropped it on the floor, and went to work on his khakis.

He had on boxer briefs underneath, and he had no intention of putting on more than that. If she didn't like it, she could sleep on the floor or hug the edge of the bed. This was how he slept. This was also how he intended to begin the process of wooing his woman back into his arms.

She'd seen him naked plenty of times. Granted, he'd added about fifty pounds of muscle since high school, but still. She knew his naked body. And he fully intended for her to reacquaint herself with it as soon as possible.

Options? Hardly. If he failed, at least he would know he'd given it his everything. If his heart broke into small pieces, he swore to himself it would have been worth it. Walking away without throwing every single punch he could was not a choice.

Bringing Ellie back to him was the only outcome he would accept, her fucking secrets and all.

As he pulled the covers back on his side of the bed and climbed under them, he was fully aware she'd watched the entire show. He didn't even pretend he was going to hug his side of the bed. He flopped right down, stretching out past the center.

She set her small hand on his arm and whispered, "I'm sorry."

He couldn't know what she meant by that. Sorry for arguing with him earlier? Sorry for leaving him years ago? Or sorry for keeping a secret from him? Didn't matter at the moment. What mattered was that she'd touched him. He took a deep breath and set his hand on top of hers.

In his mind, he heard the sound of a bell, like the one used in a boxing ring to start the fight.

Round one.

He metaphorically put up his dukes, took a breath, and started the match.

He scooted toward her, wiggled his arm under her shoulders, and hauled her closer until he had her spooned against his chest.

He gritted his teeth. She felt so good. So right. His Ellie. Exactly the same and yet totally different. Her body was softer. Rounder. Curvier. Her chest made him drool. When had she grown those damn tits?

Under her physical improvements was the same girl he fell in love with at fifteen. She sank into him the same way. She sighed as he tucked an arm under her breasts, letting the weight of them rest against his forearm.

She wore some sort of tank top. It was tight. That was all he knew. It wouldn't matter if she wore a sack, she would still be sexy. Tank top. Lingerie. Nothing. All heart stopping.

He brought his lips to her temple and kissed her. "I missed you."

"Noah…" she warned.

"Don't worry. I'm clear on the rules. Let's make some memories. If they have to last a lifetime, they better be good."

She was stiff in his arms for a few moments as if he'd shocked her with his decision. Finally, she blew out a breath and relaxed. "Okay."

He had so many cards to play. More than a full deck. Partially because he knew things about her no one else would ever know. He would use all of his knowledge to its full extent. Starting now. As if subconsciously and absentmindedly, he gently stroked his thumb back and forth on the underside of her breast.

Her breath hitched, and her fingers wrapped around his forearm, tightening. She didn't move, however, or say a word. Either she didn't want him to stop, or she was still wondering if he was aware of what he was doing.

There was no way to control his body's reaction to her, so his dick instantly stiffened, but he ignored it. His intention was going to be to woo Ellie until she couldn't say no to him. Make her beg him. He was not going to have sex with her until then. Certainly not tonight.

Tonight, he was going to hold her body close and drive her insane with his proximity. Tomorrow, he would spring into action.

Ellie was his. She had always been his. It was time to remind her of that and take her back.

～

Ellie woke to the sound of the shower. It took her a moment to orient to her surroundings, and then everything that had happened in the last twenty-four hours flooded back.

She rolled onto her side and scanned the room. Noah was definitely behind the closed bathroom door in the shower. His suitcases were no longer on the floor next to the bed, which meant he had undoubtedly unpacked them and put them in the closet. Her stuff was still a disaster, both suitcases open and spilling out the sides.

She wondered how he had managed to unpack so quietly that he didn't wake her.

The water turned off, and she waited for him to reappear, knowing it would be best if she was still lying on the bed. His body was going to make her knees weak.

Sure enough, he opened the door thirty seconds later. Steam spilled out into the room. He had the towel wrapped low on his hips, but his chest was still glistening with water.

He smiled broadly at her. "Sorry. I didn't want to

wake you, but I was getting hungry. There's a breakfast buffet that's calling my name."

She let her gaze roam up and down his body, ignoring his declaration. He was the singularly most fit human she knew. And he'd held her last night with all that strength and muscle.

She had to squeeze her thighs together under the blanket at the memory. Spending seven days with Noah was going to be hell on her nerves. And her libido. Because no way was she going to have sex with him.

She should probably point that out so there would be no expectations and no misunderstanding. It was one thing to vacation with the only man she'd ever loved. She might live through the trip. But she would not live through letting him into her body. It would destroy her.

He turned around and opened a drawer. His back side was even better than his front. His ass was firm and tight. She wanted to grab it with both hands and toss the towel away so she could admire it. His back was rippling with the same muscular outline as his front. A tattoo on his left shoulder blade drew her attention. The Navy SEAL Trident. Not surprising.

A second tattoo peeked out of the top of his towel, mostly obscured because it dipped too low. She'd give anything to see it, but she wasn't about to ask. "How long are you on leave?" That question was far more suitable, and it was time she got to know him a little better. Start with the basics.

He turned toward her, holding a pair of boxer briefs. "I retired last week."

She sat up. "Seriously? I didn't know."

He shrugged. "How would you know?"

"Why'd you retire?"

"I served two tours. It was enough. I'm worn out. It's strenuous work. I'm ready to find a nice boring civilian job." He reached for the corner of the towel next to his hip.

If he drops the towel…

Yep. He fucking dropped the towel. Damn him. He was not playing fair. He was also speaking, but she only caught something about having served two tours and being tired.

His cock was semi-hard and magnificent. Significantly larger than she remembered. He was totally playing her, ignoring the fact that she was licking her lips, her gaze locked on his package as he stepped into the briefs and then tugged them over his hips. "Ellie?"

She jerked her gaze up to his.

He was smirking. "I just asked you if you wanted to come with me."

She narrowed her gaze. "I think we need to establish a few boundaries."

He tipped his head to one side. "I thought we agreed to disagree about the past and have an enjoyable vacation."

"We did. But that isn't going to include sex. If that's a deal breaker, you need to reevaluate." Perhaps she should have made herself clearer last night.

He climbed onto the bed, one knee at a time and crawled toward her like a tiger. When he reached her side, hovering over her, she dropped onto her back to put more space between them.

He ignored her efforts, closed the distance, and kissed her lips. Not gently. Not briefly. A full-fledged kiss that made her nipples stiffen and her panties wet. She flattened her hands on his chest as soon as she could get them to obey commands and gave him a shove.

Noah was manipulating her. And she knew he could do it if she let him. She had always been a sucker for his touch.

When he finally released her lips, not in any way affected by her weak push, he smiled down at her. "Who said anything about sex?"

She rolled her eyes.

He climbed back off the bed, leaving her panting, and reached for a pair of khaki shorts. As he stepped into those, he spoke again. "This room is small. The bathroom is smaller. It's also really hot in there after you shower. No way am I going to stand in that crowded space and try to get dressed."

Her attention was riveted to his abs now.

"You've seen me naked lots of times, Ellie. I'm still the same man. Surely you can handle a little nudity. Or did you become a prude since high school?" He met her gaze.

She had, actually. His words hit closer to home than he knew. The last thing she wanted to do was admit how nonexistent her love life was. Ever. She would take that secret to the grave with the rest of her growing pile. Pride.

"No, I didn't become a prude. Don't be ridiculous. I'm just saying we're not going to sleep together, so I would appreciate it if you keep your private parts in your pants."

He chuckled as he tugged a white T-shirt over his head. "If you don't want to have sex, I can respect that. I'd certainly never pressure a woman to fuck me, even if she already had numerous times in the past. I'm a gentleman. But don't try to make that my problem, Ellie."

"What's that supposed to mean?" she asked as she pushed to sitting again and climbed off the opposite side of the bed.

"It means you're a big girl. Seeing a naked man surely doesn't cause you to change your convictions. If you can't keep your panties on simply because I'm getting dressed, then I'd say you're the one with a problem. Not me." He punctuated that last sentence by smoothing down his shirt and then lifting his eyebrows.

She groaned, stomped around the bed, and shoved past him. She needed to pee. She needed a cold shower. She needed a head examination.

"You want me to wait for you?" he shouted through the door.

"No." One word. Succinct. It would be better if he left the room so she could shower and get dressed in peace.

"Okay. I'll be on the lido deck eating breakfast, then. I'll try to get a table near where we were last night. If you want to join me. No pressure. I'll take a book."

She grabbed her toothbrush, not releasing a breath

until she heard the door snick shut. Alone. Finally. The oxygen in the room was going to be very depleted every time they were both in the cramped space.

She should have told Karla to book them a suite. Of course, knowing now what she hadn't known at the time, Karla probably would have ignored her request in order to force Noah and Ellie into a tight space.

Karla had a big heart and she meant well. Ellie loved her. But right now, she wanted to wring her neck for interfering like this. Karla didn't know all the facts. This relationship wasn't repairable. It never would be.

As soon as Ellie stepped under the hot water, she realized she had a new problem. She was going to spend the entire week aroused with almost no opportunity to do anything about it. This was her moment. She was going to have to learn to masturbate in a hurry in the shower.

Masturbating to thoughts of Noah in the shower wasn't a new concept. She was incredibly familiar with her hand between her legs. She should also be able to accomplish her goal quite fast since she now had the added benefit of seeing him in the flesh for the last twenty-four hours. His body that had done nothing but improve with age. His muscles that had grown ridiculously larger. His cock... Dammit.

She closed her eyes as she slid her fingers down to toy with her clit. Her mouth fell open, and her head tipped back. The shower was small, so the spray of water was impossible to avoid. Weak legs threatened not to support her, so she planted one hand on the wall.

Yeah, it didn't take long. She could still feel his

thumb grazing the underside of her breast last night. In fact, she flattened her chest to the wall, needing the pressure against her nipples.

Gasping, she thrust two fingers into her pussy and then dragged them back out to flick over her clit again. She hadn't brought a vibrator on a vacation with Karla, but it didn't seem she would need one anyway. She had new material to work with in her head. And that material would increase by the hour.

Picturing him standing naked in their cabin just a few minutes ago was all she needed to tip over the edge. A brief scream escaped her lips before she realized what she'd done.

Panting, she eased the pressure of her fingers while she rode out the orgasm. Two realizations came to mind. There was no way she could masturbate when he was in the room because she couldn't stop herself from crying out when she came. And, sadly, there was also no way she could guarantee he wouldn't walk into the cabin at any given moment.

Which meant, unfortunately, she couldn't do this every day.

She grabbed the shampoo with shaky fingers, squeezed some into her hand, and then lifted her arms to massage her scalp.

Emotion welled up inside her, uninvited. Probably do to the raw state of her nerves after that intense orgasm and the fact that she was so totally screwed.

CHAPTER 5

Noah vowed to leave Ellie alone for the morning. He knew he was toying with her emotions. He also knew he could push her too far. He'd done a number on her that morning. It was time to retreat a while and make her wonder where he was.

Not that he'd hidden. He claimed a lounge chair by the pool, took off his T-shirt, and leaned back to soak in the sun. It was impossible to force his body to relax. Or his mind. Both were on edge.

Ellington Gorman had slept in his arms. He'd never had her for an entire night like that. They'd been boyfriend and girlfriend for almost three years in high school. They were each other's firsts in many things. Even kissing.

The entire school had labeled them the couple most likely to marry and never divorce. People teased at graduation that they'd see them in ten years at the reunion. There had been bets placed on how many kids they would have and even what they might name them.

The teasing had never bothered Noah. It hadn't bothered Ellie either. They agreed. He'd loved her fiercely. To hell with the naysayers who said young love couldn't survive the test of time. Theirs could. He'd never doubted it for a moment.

And then she had shocked him.

He replayed every second of that day and later that night. He'd done this a thousand times until he'd forced himself to stop the nonsense years ago. Now it was all coming back, and he started it again.

She'd been distant the morning of their graduation. Off. He hadn't been able to put his finger on it. She'd gone through the motions, smiled for the cameras, tossed her cap in the air alongside him. But he'd known she had something on her mind.

When he questioned her, she blew him off. The stadium had been crowded. Normally, he wouldn't have let her get away with keeping something like that to herself, but too many demands were placed on them from the school, their parents, and their friends.

So, he'd given her space, hoping she would eventually snap out of the melancholy. She had not.

Later that night, they'd gone to a party at Layton's house. Dozens of kids had been at that party. Ellie had arrived separate, claiming she needed to spend some time with her parents.

When she arrived, he'd known something was very, very wrong. Instead of showing up in full makeup and one of her cute dresses, she'd been wearing jeans. He was sure she'd been crying. Her face was flushed. Her makeup had rubbed off as if she'd splashed water on her cheeks moments before. She was wringing her hands.

He'd rushed toward her, his excitement and smile fading. "Baby, what's wrong?"

When she nodded over her shoulder, he followed her outside. She led him to her car and leaned against the side, not meeting his gaze. Without pretense, she jumped right in. "I think we should break up."

Stunned, he'd staggered backward. "What? Ellie, what are you talking about?" His heart had raced as he forced himself back into her space and cupped her shoulders.

She wouldn't lift her gaze. Instead, she sobbed. "I can't do this."

"Do what?"

"Stay with you. It'll be too hard. You're going into the navy. You need to focus on that. I'll just be the girlfriend at home. Your new friends will harass you about having a steady girlfriend."

"That's crazy, Ellie." He'd tried to lift her chin, but she'd resisted.

Shaking her head, she'd continued. "No. It's not. It's reality. We're kidding ourselves. No one can survive this kind of separation. We're eighteen. I can't expect you to go to boot camp and stay faithful to me."

That last part had stung the most. He'd never cheated on her. Never. He'd never even thought about it. Not once. And he'd known he never would. The idea that she would even suggest such a thing hurt. "Ellie…"

She'd lifted her gaze finally. "I'm breaking up with you, Noah."

He'd shaken his head. "No. I won't let you."

"You don't have a choice. Go. Follow your dream. Fight for our country. I know you'll be the best damn SEAL who ever lived." She'd reached back and opened her car door.

He hadn't been able to process everything quick enough. In seconds, she'd slipped out of his hands and into her car. Moments later, she'd been gone from him forever.

Noah hadn't gone back into the party. Instead, he'd staggered to his own car and sat in the front seat for a long time. Eventually, he'd driven to an empty parking lot and continued to sit. Alone. Staring into space. Seeing nothing. Feeling everything.

When the sun came up, he'd driven to her parents' home. But she was not there. They were also frantically trying to locate her. She had wiped out her bank account, taken her clothes, and disappeared. According to Layton, she'd been gone for weeks before returning home a shell of the person she'd been before. She'd started college that fall, kept in touch with Karla, but she hadn't spoken of their breakup.

The devastation had been real, and it marred every moment of Noah's enlistment. It took months, years really, for him to recover. He faked it as best he could, making friends and spending leave with his buddies. But he'd never gotten over Ellie. He'd known in his heart he never would.

And now she was here. On this ship. In his cabin.

At least her body was. Her stubborn self was keeping a distance between them that made it seem like she was miles away when she was just feet away from him or right in his arms.

There was a wall around her. It had cracks, but it was thick. He wasn't sure he could climb over it. He doubted he could break it even if he had a grenade.

His heart was likely to get broken all over again this week. But he had to try. He would try his best. There were no other options, he reminded himself.

It was do or die. If he'd learned one thing in the last twenty-four hours, it was that he had nothing to lose. Seeing her. Touching her. Holding her. Everything about her reinforced his knowledge that she was it for him.

She had the power to destroy him. But she also held the only key to his future. He wouldn't have another woman. Ellie or no one. So, he would give this everything he had in him.

If he lost her for good, it wouldn't be for lack of trying. He would never look back and wonder what if…

He took a deep breath and blew it out, trying to relax. Nothing worked. His mind never stopped plotting.

A shadow came over him, and he opened his eyes to find Ellie standing next to his chair. She was wearing a skimpy white bikini, a sheer white cover-up—that covered up nothing—and white flip-flops.

Her hair was up in a messy bun, and sunglasses blocked his view of her green eyes. She smiled down at him. "You were hard to find."

She was looking…

He pushed to a sitting position and lifted the back of the lounge chair so he could lean back. "Sorry. I dozed off. Did you have breakfast?"

"Yes." She glanced around, chewing on her bottom lip.

He set his feet down on either side of the lounge chair and patted the space between his legs. "Sit. I'm sure it will be impossible to find another chair right now."

She lowered to the far end of the seat and set her bag down between them.

He leaned over it, peering down. "What all do you have in there? It looks heavy."

"Not really. Sunscreen. A few books. My phone. A hat. Normal stuff."

"A *few* books? How many can you read at once?"

"Never know which one I might be in the mood for." She reached inside and pulled out the sunscreen. "Did you put any on? You're gonna burn in this sun."

"Baby, I've seen sun in the last ten years that puts the Gulf of Mexico to shame. I think I'll live."

"Fine. But don't call me when your face is all cut up with a dozen scars from having patches of cancer removed."

He leaned back. "Are you saying you'd judge me by my looks?" It was too easy to tease her.

"Never. Don't twist my words."

He reached out, grabbed her wrist, and wrenched the sunscreen from her hand. "Turn around."

She hesitated, and then undoubtedly decided she had no other options.

Score.

As soon as she turned to face away from him, he grabbed her hips and drew her backward closer to him.

She squeaked. "Noah. Jeez."

"You planning to wear this flimsy wrap, or you want me to put protection on your back?"

She shot him a look over her shoulder, but she tugged the translucent cover-up over her head.

For a second, he simply stared. The only thing on her back was the thin tie holding her breasts in place. And from what he'd seen of the front of her, the two triangles covered hardly more than her nipples. She was going to be difficult to ignore. Not just for him but any other man who walked by.

Finally, he popped the top of the tube, squirted a generous portion of lotion on his palm, and rubbed his hands together. He tucked both lips between his teeth before he set his palms on her shoulders to keep from making a sound.

Heaven.

Her smooth skin hadn't seen sunlight in a long time. He knew from past experience she would be a lovely shade of bronze by the end of the week, but not today. Right now her skin was pale, several shades lighter than his.

He spread the sunscreen down her shoulder blades, making sure he pushed the thin string out of the way as he went so that she didn't get a burn line across her back when it shifted. When he got to the tiny bikini bottom that barely covered her butt, he had to stifle a moan. He'd give anything to slide his hands lower, into her suit, and cup her ass.

She was living dangerously with matching strings holding her bikini bottom together on both sides. One tug of the little ties and she'd be naked.

He worked his hands back up her body, making sure no white smudges of lotion were noticeable, and then he slid his fingers over her shoulders to reach her chest.

She batted his hands away. "I think I can reach the front."

He leaned closer so his lips were inches from her ear. "Can't blame a guy for trying."

She twisted around, face red. "Did you miss the part where I said we're not having sex?"

He furrowed his brow as if he were offended. "Who said anything about sex?" he repeated for the second time that day. "You're the one who keeps bringing it up. It must be on your mind. I don't think rubbing lotion into your skin counts as sex."

She yanked the sunscreen from the bench beside them, ignoring his comment, and proceeded to rub it into the rest of her body.

He watched. He'd watch this show any day. It wasn't quite as good as doing it himself, but almost.

"Have you been in the pool?" she asked. "Is the water cold?"

He shook his head. "Not yet. I was thinking we could head toward the hot tubs in the adult-only section at the front when you got here. Might be less crowded."

She nodded. "I'd like to lie in the sun for a while

first. I feel like I already need a nap, even though all I've done is shower and eat breakfast."

"It's vacation. You can nap if you want. How about if I get up so you can relax on this chair? They're at a premium. You can't move or you'll lose it. I'll go find out what kind of excursions they're offering at the first port." He swung one leg over the chair and stood before leaning the back down flat for her again.

Ellie lowered herself onto her back and then shielded her eyes with one hand to block the sun enough to see him. "How about snorkeling?"

"Sounds good. I'll see what they have." He considered walking off without saying anything else, but he couldn't resist tempting her, so instead, he leaned over her, set his hand on the arm of the chair on his opposite side, and kissed her lips gently. "Be back soon."

Later that afternoon, they were in the casino, and Ellie couldn't stop giggling. She had a pair of dice between her palms and she was about to toss them down the craps table yet again.

Several people were watching her play because Lady Luck seemed to be on her side today. She was only vaguely aware of the growing crowd, however, because every time she lifted her gaze, it landed on Noah. He was smiling at her. Indulgently. One arm crossed over his chest, the opposite elbow resting in his hand while he stroked his chin with his fingers.

She didn't think he had ever once looked down at

the table to see what numbers she threw. It was possible he hadn't even realized she was on a winning streak. His gaze burned into her.

And it felt so damn good.

She remembered that heated gaze, so many snapshots in her mind. He'd always loved it when she laughed, when she was truly happy. It had been a long time since she'd felt that emotion so strongly. Honestly, she didn't think she'd been this carefree in over a decade. Not since the two of them had climbed into the back seat of his car about a month before she broke up with him and fogged up the windows with their lovemaking. She'd drawn silly faces on the glass with her toes as they basked in the afterglow.

She flushed at the memory as she glanced down and tossed the dice. She had no idea what numbers she threw because she lifted her gaze back to Noah immediately. But the crowd was clapping, so it must have been good.

She could still feel the intensity of his gaze boring into her as the dice found their way back into her hands. She was shaking as she threw them one more time, not from the stress of gambling but from the heated stare from Noah. A collaborative sigh from the crowd informed her she'd finally crapped out.

Suddenly, Noah lurched toward her, grabbed her around the waist, and flattened his front against her back. She giggled as she collected her chips. He rocked her back and forth as they backed away from the table. His lips were on her neck, nibbling a path to her ear.

After flicking his tongue over the sensitive lobe, he

whispered, "God, I love to hear you laugh. The world disappears when that soft sound fills the room."

Heat raced up her chest, and she knew her cheeks were bright red. She hugged his arms around her waist and sighed as her eyes slid closed. She wanted to remember this moment for years to come. Maybe it would be a pleasant memory when times were tough.

Or maybe it would destroy her.

CHAPTER 6

Ellie was slowly losing her mind. She stood in the tiny bathroom that evening, staring at her reflection in the mirror and wondering how she was going to survive six more days of Noah Seager.

He looked fantastic. He smelled fantastic. He stroked her skin every time he walked near her. He kissed her neck or ear or mouth or cheek or forehead or hand or arm as often as he could.

Yeah, she was going to lose it, and she suspected it was all part of some giant plan he had to break her.

"We better hurry if you want to make the 8:15 dinner, Ellie." His voice was just loud enough to reach her through the door.

She glanced at her watch. She had less than half an hour. She didn't need it, though. She was ready except for getting dressed. Makeup and hair were done.

She stepped out of the bathroom wrapped in her

towel. "I only need about five minutes. Can you step out of the room so I can get dressed?"

He grinned at her. This was when she noticed he had dressed while she was in the bathroom. He wore gray dress pants and a light blue dress shirt with a black tie and black loafers. He looked better than she'd ever seen him, and she nearly swallowed her tongue.

The breath left her lungs while she took him in. Her hand shook where she held the towel closed. Her breasts grew heavier. And her pussy wept. *Wept.*

If her body didn't stop betraying her, she would end up naked under him before the end of day one. And that was not an option.

"Ellie, I'm not going to stand in the hall while you dress. But I'll go on the balcony and face the water as a compromise. However, if you think I don't remember every inch of your body, you're sadly mistaken. Plus, I saw all but about two inches earlier this afternoon, along with every other person on this ship." He winked at her and then stepped outside.

The cooler breeze hit her and calmed her racing heart. Marginally. She stared at Noah's back for a few seconds, wondering if he would truly honor her wishes or spin around as soon as she dropped the towel.

One thing was for sure, she had no options, so she needed to hurry and put her dress on before she tempted fate.

She grabbed a pale blue dress out of the closet, ridiculously thinking it would match his shirt nicely. Why she thought this was necessary was beyond her. But she did it anyway.

After a quick glance to find Noah leaning his elbows on the balcony railing, she set the towel on the bed and quickly slid the silky dress over her head. Holding the bodice up, she considered at least putting on a thong and then decided against it. This dress hadn't been made for undergarments. It had no back and clung to her hips in a way that would tell everyone what she was wearing underneath.

Unfortunately for her, she hadn't planned this trip with Noah in mind. She'd planned a girls' vacation with Karla. One in which she'd intended to let her hair down, dress in fantastic clothes, and at least get men to notice her even if she hadn't intended to give them the time of day.

She was still a woman. Stubborn perhaps, but she enjoyed when a man gave her a double take just as much as the next gal. Too bad she was now stuck on this ship with sexy clothes and a man she'd love to ravage.

She reached behind her neck to tie the two ends of the fabric that would hold the dress up and quickly realized the task was going to be difficult to accomplish on her own. The dress would fall unnaturally if she tried to fasten it with her arms in the air.

Damn Karla.

She padded toward the sliding door. "Would you tie the back for me, please?" She was holding the straps with one hand at the base of her neck, her other hand reaching for the doorframe, so she wouldn't trip over the lip that led to the outside.

Noah turned around. He pushed off the railing and took one step toward her and then stopped. His gaze widened and then swept rapidly up and down her body. He was breathing heavily.

Great.

Bad dress choice. Not that she had better ones.

"Jesus, Ellie. You look beautiful."

She blushed. It wasn't avoidable. Even though she really didn't want him to see her that way, it felt good. Really good. He was eyeing her with an intensity she hadn't seen even in high school. "Thank you," she whispered.

She turned around slowly and shook the silky fabric at her neck to get him to take it from her.

His hands landed on her shoulders, his warmth seeping into her skin and bringing goose bumps to the surface. When he slid them up to her neck and took the two ends, she released her grip and lowered her arms to her sides.

Noah slowly tied the silk, giving it just enough of a tug to make the dress land right. When he was finished, he reached up and removed the clip she'd carefully placed in her hair.

"Hey," she blurted. "It took me forever to get that right."

He wrapped his palms around her biceps, leaned in close, and kissed the sensitive spot behind her ear. "I like it down better," he whispered.

She couldn't breathe. If circumstances were different. If life hadn't derailed her train car fourteen years ago. If she were a weaker woman… she would say fuck dinner, turn around, and jump into his arms.

The truth was, Ellie would give just about anything

to have him inside her. The intensity in his gaze melted her resolve. The way he breathed on her neck and stroked her skin made her knees weak. Who cared if his every move was a calculated effort to get her into his bed?

Yeah, she would give just about anything. But there was one thing she would not give, and that piece of information was critical and would ruin everything.

She swallowed her emotion, fortified herself against his touch, and stepped out of his embrace. "I just need my shoes, and I'll be ready," she murmured in a husky voice she didn't recognize as her own.

She scrambled across the room, found her wedges in the closet, and slipped them on without looking back. When she stood, shaking out her messy hair, she found him holding both sides of the glass doorframe, his broad body leaning into the room. His gaze was heated like it took every effort to contain himself.

"Ready?" she asked, hoping to spur him into action.

He nodded slowly, stepped inside, and shut the sliding door. Swiping their keycards off the desk, he stuffed both of them in his pocket and opened the door to the hallway.

The air was thick with sexual tension. She knew he felt it too.

She was so screwed.

Noah sat across from Ellie at a private table in the elegant dining room, silently thanking Karla for requesting they not be seated for the week with ten other people.

He wanted Ellie all to himself.

She was fidgeting, which she'd done from the moment they took their seats.

Good. He loved that he was under her skin. He also loved that her nipples were so obviously hard under the thin material of her silky dress. He sat as casually as possible, spinning his glass of wine around by the stem, not taking his gaze off her. Who would?

Her dress fit her perfectly as if it were made specifically for her. He'd nearly choked when he'd first seen her as he turned around on the balcony. He'd known instantly she was bare under the soft silk. The material in the front covered nothing but her tits, her back was bare, and the skirt flared at her hips to land mid-thigh. He'd considered running his hands up her legs until her knees buckled.

She was divine. Elegant. Sophisticated. But also playful. Way out of his league.

She lifted her gin and tonic and took another sip. It was half-finished, and they hadn't even had their first course yet.

"We match," he pointed out.

She tipped her head to one side for a second and then glanced down at her dress and then across at his shirt. "Yeah. We do."

They didn't match at all. Except for their colors. Those did appear coordinated. But she looked like a movie star. He looked like a guy in a suit. "Photographers are going to snag us in the hallway."

"Probably." She took another sip.

He lifted his glass and drank from it. The flavors burst in his mouth, making him smile. "This is a very good Merlot, if you want to try it."

She wrinkled up her nose. "No, thanks. I never developed a taste for wine. Not even sweet wine."

He leaned forward, setting his elbows on the table. "Maybe you haven't had a good one before."

She pointed at his glass. "I know that's dry. Gross."

He chuckled. "Okay. More for me."

"I'll stick with the gin and tonic," she said, lifting her glass toward him. "Especially if it's Bombay Sapphire. It goes down a little too smoothly. Don't let me drink more than two of these, or you'll be carrying me back to the room."

"Hmmm. And you think that warning is going to help your case?"

She tipped her eyes to the ceiling but met his gaze with a grin. "Fair point."

Their appetizers arrived, the waiter making a flourishing motion as he set them down. Renaldo. He was from Spain. He would be with them all week.

Noah lifted his gaze. "Thank you. That looks delicious."

Ellie picked up her spoon and dipped it in her vichyssoise. She moaned around the first taste. If she did that often, he would gladly order her three more gin and tonics and be happy carrying her back to the room.

Not that he'd take advantage of her when she wasn't sober, but he would enjoy the opportunity to hold her sweet body close as he carried her to their cabin.

Noah picked up a shrimp, dipped it in the cocktail sauce, and savored the flavor. "We are totally not going to miss any more dinners."

"Agreed."

"Tell me about your job," he inquired as they finished their first course.

She didn't answer him right away. Instead, she wiped her lips and stared at some spot across the room. Finally, she met his gaze. "Okay, here's the prepared speech I intended to give you."

He furrowed his brow. "Okay…"

"It's demanding and exhausting and challenging and exciting all at the same time. I work long hours. I make a lot of money. I have saved most of it over the years. It's cutthroat. Anyone who does it for too many years will die early and alone."

He lifted his brows now. "Shit. I can't tell if you love it or hate it."

"Both."

"Wait, you said that was a prepared speech. What's the version you didn't share?"

She lifted her glass to her lips, the ice tinkling as she finished the drink.

Noah took it from her hand, lifted it toward a passing waiter, and set it on the table. Someone would bring her another one. He reached for that same hand and held it in his larger one on the table. "Talk to me."

She licked her lips. "You have a way of making me say things I didn't intend to divulge."

He smiled broadly. *Thank fuck. If I'm lucky enough, she'll lead me to the gold mine eventually.*

"I quit on Friday."

He jerked in his seat. Shock didn't begin to describe his reaction. "What? Seriously? Why?"

She shrugged. "Same reasons you listed for getting out of the navy. It was enough. I'm worn out. It's strenuous work." She repeated his reasons for leaving the SEALs verbatim.

"Are you okay with it?" he asked. She had devoted a decade to Wall Street.

"Yes. Totally. A little nervous. Uncertain. I have no idea what I'm going to do next, but *yes*." She sat up straighter, adding one nod of her head for emphasis.

"You didn't line up a new job?"

She shook her head. "Nope. I'm going to wing it when I get back. Find myself. Start over."

"Don't you have an apartment in New York City?" How was she going to pay the rent? He didn't care. He was just curious. Hell, if he had his way, she would leave that apartment and run off with him to a quiet mountain cabin where they could make up for lost time, fucking so often that they couldn't get out of bed.

If there were a God.

"I do. Did you miss the part where I said I made a lot of money? I'm good. I can take my time finding something else."

Find me.

He lifted his wine, finished the glass, and set it down.

Less than a moment later, their bartender arrived, set a new glass in front of Ellie, and refilled Noah's. He swiped Ellie's finished drink from the table and left so fast his presence had been a blur.

"I don't know what to say," he responded. "That's... not what I expected."

"Yeah, I know." She extricated her hand from under his and leaned back. "I haven't even said it out loud until now. My parents don't even know. No one does."

"Why? Do you think people will be disappointed?"

She ran her finger around the rim of her glass, thinking. "Not really. No. Just shocked. I was too tired to get into it with anyone. I just wanted to get to the port and start my vacation. I was looking forward to a girls' week with Karla. I haven't seen her in five years. I thought we'd laugh and catch up and relax and eat and play and sun and swim and so many other things." Her voice trailed off. She lifted her gaze. "I'm gonna kill her."

He smiled. "I'll kill Layton while you do Karla, and we'll bury the bodies in their own yard."

"It's a plan."

He cleared his throat. "I'm sorry about your vacation with Karla. I'm sure you're disappointed."

She shrugged. Took another drink. Her eyes were serious and warm when she looked at him again. "I know this might sound confusing, and I'm probably a bitch for saying it out loud, but..."

"Go on," he encouraged. If she stopped there, he would not be able to breathe properly again.

She took a deep breath, lifted her hand, reached across the table, and cupped his fresh-shaved cheek. "I know we got off to a shocked and rocky start, but the truth is I wouldn't trade this accidental trip with you for anything in the world. I'm a selfish bitch. I'm super clear on that. But I want this anyway.

79

"I want to spend every second with you. I want to soak in your excitement for life. I want to eat and sunbathe and snorkel and shop and drink and go to shows and sleep in your arms. I want all of that for seven days. It's all I'll ever get. I know it. I realize I can't have more. But I'm so damn happy I could cry."

He sucked in a breath, stunned silent. When he reached up with his hand to cover hers over his cheek, he slid his face to kiss her palm. Her words meant the world to him. They told him everything he needed to know. She loved him. She'd never stopped loving him. She'd even loved him while she was breaking his heart fourteen years ago.

What if she never told him why she'd left him that day? Could he live with it for the rest of his life? Could he somehow decide that his feelings for her were so much more important than whatever made her dump him that he could let it go, forgive her, and move on?

Twenty-four hours ago he would have said fuck no. But his shield was crumbling.

Not that it mattered. He wasn't the only player in this game. She would also have to agree to such an arrangement. He doubted she could. That was why she said everything she'd just said. She was going to leave him at the end of the week with no discussion.

He held her hand closer, closed his eyes, and inhaled the scent of her palm. "Why, baby?" It was all he could manage. It came out croaked. A whisper.

She pulled her hand back, took a breath, and set her napkin in her lap. "Our dinner is here," she stated softly.

Sure enough, Noah jerked his attention to his left to

find Renaldo waiting patiently for them to part so he could set their plates down. He was silent as he did so, as unobtrusive as possible, and then he was gone.

Noah found his appetite had vanished. His throat was dry. He didn't think he could swallow.

Why did she have to be so stubborn?

Couldn't she see how much he loved her? Had always loved her?

She shuddered, her entire body shaking. And then she forced a smile. "Enough gloom. Let's eat and go to the comedy show."

How she could bounce back like that was beyond him, but if she could do it, he would find a way to join her. He had no choice. She had him by the balls. He would do anything for her. He'd walk to the ends of the earth if she asked him.

Could he also let go of the past?

CHAPTER 7

Ellie was beyond aware of Noah's hand at the small of her back as they returned to their room several hours later. She'd enjoyed another gin and tonic at the comedy show, but three wasn't going to put her over the edge considering how much time had elapsed and how much food she'd eaten.

She felt relaxed. Happy. Her face was tight from laughing so hard. The comedian had been hilarious.

Noah had never stopped touching her. His hand was always on her somewhere. Her back, her shoulder, her thigh. He'd even held her hand several times. He'd been possessive, sat closer to her than necessary, whispered in her ear.

No one around could have believed she wasn't having sex with him. She was well aware they presented as the perfect couple, perhaps even two people who were getting engaged on this trip.

It had been so long since she'd dated anyone, let

alone someone who doted on her like Noah did. He clearly adored her.

It felt so good. She couldn't bring herself to stop him. She wanted him with every fiber of her being. Her body was on fire. Her pussy had been so wet for so many hours it was a wonder she hadn't left evidence of it on her dress. She hadn't looked.

She had no idea how she was going to keep her distance from him for another hour, let alone the entire week. He was doing his best to wear her down, and he was good. Damn good.

She was playing with fire.

They reached their cabin, and he extracted their keycards from his pocket, opened the door, and let them in. He dropped both cards on the desk as she wandered toward the balcony. She needed air. Desperately.

She slid the door open, aware of Noah behind her, tugging on his tie and then tossing it on the bed. He opened the first few buttons of his shirt next. She watched this through the mirrored glass door. The only lights in the room were those coming from the moon and a dim light above the bed.

She held on to the doorframe with one hand and reached down with the other to remove her shoes. And then she stepped out onto the balcony and sucked in oxygen.

Noah followed her. He'd removed his shoes too. He stepped up behind her, crowding her at the balcony. His hands reached around both sides of her and planted on the railing.

She pressed against the Plexiglas until there was no more room to escape him.

He set his chin on her shoulder.

They stared out at the night for a long time. The wind whipped her hair in his face. He said nothing.

The sounds of the engine and the waves soothed. The scent of salt filled the air. The cool breeze did its part to tamp down her ardor, but it wasn't enough.

Ellie was aware of every inch of the vibrant man behind her. His cock pressed against her butt. His pecs nestled across her shoulders as if they fit together like puzzle pieces.

They did.

They always had.

Why did stupid shit have to get in the way and ruin everything? What a cruel world.

Noah kissed her neck until she tilted her head to one side to give him better access. His hands came from the railing to her biceps. They smoothed up and down, drawing her into his warmth while he continued to torment her with his lips.

When he slid his hands to her back and let them glide slowly around until he cupped her breasts beneath the silk of her dress, her head fell back against his shoulder, and she gasped. "Noah…"

He palmed her heavy breasts and then stroked his thumbs over her nipples.

She rose up on her tiptoes, gripping the balcony with her fists. Her tight buds grew stiffer as he worked them. His touch was nothing like the fumbling ministrations of a teenage Noah. He was a man now. He knew what he was doing. And he was destroying her resolve.

He squeezed one breast enough to make her breath catch and then took advantage of her complete loss of brain cells to slide his other hand across her belly and lower to cup her mound.

She cried out.

His middle finger found her clit easily through the thin layer of silk. Undoubtedly encouraged by her reaction, he let that hand slip closer to her core and then slowly pressed against her entrance.

He didn't even bother to remove the material impediment, which made his actions even hotter. Instead, he pushed the silk up into her. Slowly. So gradually it was almost imperceptible. Except there was no way in hell anyone alive could miss a second of his torment.

She moaned, her hands gripping the railing as an orgasm rushed to the surface. She couldn't do this. She was taking advantage of him. Or he was taking advantage of her. She didn't know which, but it would be too intense for her to shatter in his arms.

She grabbed his wrist. "Noah…"

He didn't continue, but he didn't pull out either. His finger was about an inch into her tight channel, her clit trapped against his palm. Another inch and she would come, screaming in the night air.

"Noah, stop. I told you we're not having sex. I meant it." If he ignored that demand, she wouldn't be able to trust him. Sex was a hard line. Sex was always a hard line for her. Even if she could permit herself to let go like that, she wouldn't. If she let him into her body, she would never get him out of her soul. He would destroy her. He had that power over her.

And it would be so much worse than she imagined because this thirty-two-year-old Noah was an improved version who knew exactly what he was doing.

His lips were on her ear again. His hand still palmed her breast. His thumb still stroked her nipple to a stiff peak. His finger still pressed into her tightness. The base of his hand still nestled against her clit.

Every inch of her was tingling with desire and the need to come.

He whispered. "I heard you, baby. I would never break your trust. I swear. But let me make you feel good. You never said anything about fooling around. If the boundary you need set between us is my cock in your pussy, you shall keep that piece of your virtue. But don't deny me the pleasure of watching you come apart in my arms. Please..."

She couldn't move. Not even to respond. His words filtered in. She understood their meaning. But she also knew he was manipulating her. He probably had a plan to do so all week, thinking he could break her down until she gave in.

He was in for an unpleasant surprise if he thought she would cave. It wasn't because she didn't want to. God knew she would be tested by him a thousand times in the next six days. But she would never lose sight of the damage fucking him would do to her.

No amount of alcohol or cajoling would penetrate that wall.

"Ellie… baby… you need the release. I'm offering it. Take it." He was at least gentleman enough to hold steady while he fought her for this small victory. He didn't push in deeper or squeeze her breast harder. He waited.

She moaned. Denying him wasn't a possibility. Instead, she pointed out the thing he needed to understand most. "If you fuck me while I'm weak, I'll never forgive you, Noah."

"I know, baby. I swear I will not. My cock won't even graze the edge of your sweet pussy until you beg me to do so. Sober and clothed."

"It won't happen."

"If you're right, I'll live." He didn't admit defeat, but he did give her an inch.

Her legs shook.

He held her closer. "May I continue?"

"Yes." The word came out on a breathy sigh.

He didn't hesitate. His finger thrust up into her, taking her dress with it.

She cried out, releasing his wrist to grab the railing again.

He pinched her nipple sharply, sending a rush of pleasure/pain down her body like an electric shock. He'd never been this dominant with her fourteen years ago. They had been hardly more than kids.

"That's it," he whispered against her ear. "Let it go, baby. Let me take you there." He pulled almost out and then thrust back in, this time with two fingers, made that much tighter insider her with her dress bunched around them.

His third thrust was deeper.

The silk was soaked. Her clit was sensitive. Her nipple ached as he released the tight pinch and switched to torment the other one.

His cock pressed against her lower back, tempting her. Making her fight against her willpower.

If she were a different person, with a different past, it would be so easy to say *yes*. To let bygones be bygones and take him deep into her body. Each stroke of his cock would be exquisite torture. She could endure it. Hell, she would love it.

But she would never recover from it.

Over and over she had to remind herself that making love to him would destroy her. And that's what it would be. They could call it sex or fucking, but it would be making love, because that's all she knew with Noah.

Because she loved him.

He sped up his thrusts, her feet nearly lifting off the floor as he fucked her tight pussy with those two fingers.

She let her head drop forward, her hair cascading around her face like a curtain. It closed her off from the world, leaving her in a dreamland where all that existed was Noah and the way he made her feel like she was the most important person in the world.

She believed him. He'd always made her feel special. But this day was bittersweet.

Suddenly, he ground his palm against her clit and rubbed it up and down.

She sucked in a breath and held it, her eyes squeezing shut as she climbed to the top of the mountain.

And then she was falling. With no warning, she crested the peak and tipped over the edge. Her entire body convulsed as he slid his fingers in and out of her, gripped her breast with his other hand, and ground his cock into her lower back.

"That's it, baby. Take what you need. You're so gorgeous when you come."

The flutters of her orgasm continued for long moments, her body jerking with every pulse. Her knees gave out.

He held her.

He held her upright through the entire experience. Even when he eased his fingers out of her pussy, he continued to cup her to keep her from sliding to the floor like a pile of goo.

Still holding her bare breast, he slid his other hand up her side until he reached her cheek. He gripped her chin loosely with his thumb and forefinger and tipped her head around to meet his. His lips closed on hers for a long kiss that would have made her weaker than she already was, except that wasn't possible.

When he broke free, he spoke against her mouth. "You always were a firecracker when you came. Sexiest woman I've ever been with. Hands down."

She stiffened slightly at the thought of him being with other women. Of course he had. He was a guy first and foremost. She'd always imagined him with a lineup of dates. He was sexy, smart, built, and kind.

That last part was no joke. Noah was the kindest man she knew. Women in every port must have fought for a piece of him.

Noah finally released her breast but only so that he could bend at the knees, lift her in his arms, and carry her back inside. He set her on her feet next to the bed, untied her dress at the nape of her neck, and let the silk fall to the floor.

She was naked before him, less than an inch between them because that was all he permitted. Her butt was against the mattress.

She considered arguing or covering herself, but instead, she got caught up in his gaze as he held her at arm's length and reverently perused her body.

"When did your sweet tits fill out like this?" he asked.

She smiled. "When I stopped being a kid and started putting on weight."

His head jerked back. "Putting on weight? I hope you're not implying for a second that you weigh too much, because that would drive me to drink."

She gripped his forearms and met his gaze. "I'm not saying that. I'm just saying I was a bit skinny in high school. Most girls are. But then we add a few pounds over the years. Before we get out of college, we usually look more like a woman. I did."

After studying her face for a moment, he reached down to pull back the covers and lowered her onto the bed. Easing her onto her back, he released her and reached for the buttons on his shirt.

His gaze never left hers while he undressed down to his boxer briefs. And then he climbed over her body, nestled his legs under the covers next to hers, and pulled the sheet over them. He immediately pulled her into his side and kissed the top of her head. "Thank you, baby. That was a gift I will never forget."

She bit her lower lip as she turned onto her side to more fully press her body into his. The only clothing between them was his briefs. His cock was rigid against her hip. She lowered her hand under the blankets, thinking to alleviate the strain. But he stopped her with a grip to her wrist. "Don't."

She hesitated. "Let me return the favor."

"Not tonight, Ellie. Another time."

She wasn't sure what to make of his request, but she was too sated and relaxed to argue. Instead, she flattened her palm on his chest and closed her eyes. Her head rested in the curve of his arm. She would spend the night inhaling his scent, listening to his breaths as they evened out, feeling the hardness of his body.

She tried to stay awake long enough to outlast him, but she was too comfortable and relaxed after that amazing orgasm to keep from closing her eyes.

He held her tighter, his arm around her shoulders, his fingers stroking the side of her breast. She didn't care that she was naked and he wore nothing but boxer briefs. It had been inevitable. She could handle this. Right? It wasn't the full deal. Just some messing around.

Third base maybe. Not a home run. That had to be the line. The rest of the lines blurred.

She could do this. Keep her resolve all week not to let him inside her. She drifted off, vowing to keep her legs together. It was the most important thing in the world. She could do it. For six more days.

Right?

CHAPTER 8

When Noah woke up the next morning, Ellie was gone from the room. He wasn't surprised to find he'd slept through her escape, considering how long he'd lain awake watching her sleep the night before.

His stiff erection wasn't the only thing that kept him up. He'd been restless. Desperate. It was unlike him to feel the way he felt about Ellie. In fourteen years he hadn't experienced anything like it since her. After two days with her, everything had fallen right back into place as if no time had passed and nothing had happened to separate them.

Except time had passed. A lot of it. And some incident he was still unaware of had broken them apart. Torn them to shreds.

They hadn't shut the blinds either night, so the morning sun was streaming into the room as it had yesterday. The sliding door was also open a few inches, permitting him to enjoy the sounds of the ocean. Their room was low enough in the ship that he could hear the waves lapping at the sides.

He ran a hand through his hair, wondering what he should do next. This entire week was like a game. Push Ellie hard enough to get her to fall in love with him again —though there was little doubt that was an issue, or ever had been. At the same time, he needed to walk the thin line of not nudging her so far that she ran from him.

He was on a roller coaster with no exit plan.

After dragging himself from the bed, he took a quick shower, dressed in board shorts, sandals, and a tank top, and headed out to find her. Or breakfast. Whichever came first.

As he left the room, he had a thought that made him smile and pick up his pace. He took a detour to the on-board florist, made his selection, and headed toward the breakfast buffet.

It turned out she was easy to locate. He filled a plate with food and then stepped out onto the deck. She was sitting on a lounge chair in the same vicinity as he'd been the day before. On purpose?

"Hey," he said as he approached. He had his plate in one hand and a single white rose in the other. He leaned over and held it out to her.

Her mouth fell open, and she flushed as she accepted the rose. "You remembered."

"How could I forget?" When they were in high school, he hadn't been able to afford elaborate flower arrangements, and one day he stopped to get her a rose, but the store was all out of red, so he'd grabbed a white

94

one. When he'd presented it to her, she'd cried. From that day forward, he surprised her as often as possible with one single white rose.

She glanced up from the book in her hand. "Thank you." Her voice was hoarse. Next, she patted the chair next to her and dragged her bag off it to the deck floor. "Saved you a seat."

"Thanks." It meant something that she'd been so thoughtful. As soon as he had his plate propped in his lap, he grabbed a piece of bacon and ate the entire thing in two bites.

Ellie glanced at his plate. "I'm going to gain twenty pounds this week."

"You and me both. No one will recognize us when we get off the ship."

"Who would be there to recognize us?" she asked. "I mean if Layton and Karla dared to show up, we would strangle them both. I quit my job, so I'm in no hurry to go home. You quit your job, so you…where are you planning to go?"

He shrugged. "I hadn't thought that far. I figured I'd spend some time with my parents in League City and then regroup and decide what I want to do next."

She nodded slowly. "I was thinking the same thing. I haven't even told my parents I quit. Hell, I didn't tell them I went on this cruise." She leaned back in her chair, her book forgotten on her lap, and stared at the sky.

She was wearing another bikini—this one navy— with a matching cover-up that was once again doing nothing to hide her assets. It was a woven mesh wrap that had more holes than material.

Noah ate the rest of his breakfast and was just about to set his plate on the floor when a waiter showed up and took it from him. As Noah situated himself on the lounge chair alongside her, she turned to face him.

Her expression was far too serious. "I think we're playing with fire, Noah."

"How do you mean?" He knew exactly what she meant, and it scared him to death.

"I mean, we're not getting back together. It's not possible. We can't go through the motions this week acting like we're a couple. We can't have a repeat of what happened last night."

He swallowed. "Why not? I had a great time. Didn't you?"

"Of course—"

He interrupted her. "Don't add a *but*. Just have fun."

She shook her head. "Don't try to make light of this. I'm being serious. I can't just take from you like that without giving."

"You didn't take anything from me, Ellie. That's ridiculous. If anything, I took from you." He sat up, swung his legs around, and leaned his elbows on his knees to face her. He lowered his voice. "I spent the entire evening falling under your spell in that sexy dress with no bra or panties. Your tits alone had me salivating before we left the room."

She paled.

"Don't misread me. You looked fucking amazing. Every man on the ship was jealous of me." He leaned even closer until inches separated their faces, his voice a whisper. "By the time we got back to the room, the only thing on my mind was getting that dress off you and putting my hands and mouth everywhere on your delectable body.

"So I crowded you. I knew immediately it was the right decision because you were so hot for me that the ocean water boiled. I've never seen anything sexier than making you come with my finger pressing that silky skirt up into your tight pussy, Ellie.

"I did that. I wanted to do it. I would do it again in a heartbeat. You enjoyed it. I loved it. Don't minimize it this morning and try to convince me it was a mistake."

"It was a mistake," she murmured.

He groaned, leaning back. It was impossible not to react to her words. She was bullshitting him, and he couldn't get her to see reason.

"It's wrong of me to lead you on like that because I don't want you to get some false sense of hope that we can get back together."

He sat up straighter and ran a hand through his hair. "You've certainly made that clear. Several times. I get it. You're not interested in a reconciliation. Fine. But don't try to pretend you're not equally as attracted to me as I am you. You can argue the points all day in your mind, but your body betrays you."

She bolted to a sitting position, swinging her legs over the side of the lounge and stuffing her book into her bag. "I think we should do different things today."

"Ellie…"

She stood, stuffed her feet into a dainty pair of silver

flip-flops and shook her head. "I'm serious. We need space. *I* need space. I'll meet you back at the room before dinner." At that, she spun around and walked off, disappearing between the people roaming around the deck.

In seconds, a female voice spoke to him from the other side of her chair. "Is this seat taken?"

"Nope. It's all yours." He leaned back, closed his eyes, and tried to slow his racing heart. Why did everything have to be so complicated?

When Ellie stepped out of the shower that night, she knew Noah was in the room. She could feel the intensity he filled every small space with before even opening the bathroom door.

Her day had been total shit. She'd gone to the trivia contest for a while but found she didn't know anything in today's category. Next, she'd joined the bingo in the giant auditorium with several hundred people over the age of sixty. After that, she'd found a quiet corner on an out-of-the-way deck and tried to read while sipping a gin and tonic. She had no idea what the book was about. Even the casino held no appeal without Noah there watching her.

After drying her hair in the cramped space, she was forced to open the door or suffocate from the humid heat in the small bathroom.

Noah was standing next to the bed, hands at his sides, gaze locked on her as if he'd been waiting for her to come out. He was dressed for dinner, which meant he'd come back earlier and showered and changed.

They both spoke at once. "I'm sorry."

She let her shoulders relax marginally. "I shouldn't have said all that. This week is no more your fault that it is mine. We didn't ask for this." She reached for the closet door, opened it, and stared at her dress selection.

"You're right," he agreed, easing up beside her. "You want me to pick one?"

She realized she was staring at her choices, knowing all of them were inappropriate for a week-long trip with a man she wasn't going to sleep with. She had purchased this wardrobe on a whim, thinking to flirt with men and relax her usual stuffy self. She never would have been able to pull it off, so it seemed ridiculous now, but she was stuck.

She chewed on her bottom lip and then met his gaze. "I didn't know I was going on a trip with you when I selected these dresses. I can't help that they're too revealing. It's kinda late for that."

He gave her a wry grin. "They aren't too revealing. They're sexy and just right. They suit you. I was being a dick earlier."

She shook her head. "No. You were right. I can't dress in fuck-me clothes and then tell you I'm off-limits."

He reached into the closet and selected a pale pink dress. It was the most sophisticated one she'd brought, but it would still hug all her curves and land not low enough on her thighs. It was meant to pick up men, not run them off. "This one. The skirt will be too tight for me to navigate it into your pussy later. It's perfect."

When she jerked her gaze to his, she found him smiling. His eyes were dancing. She rolled hers and snagged it from him.

"See? You'll be totally safe in that one. I'll wait on the balcony. Let me know when you want me to zip it up." With that, he turned around and stepped outside.

Like last night, she stared at his back while she dropped the towel and grabbed a bra and panty set. Pink, to match the dress. She quickly stepped into the thong and then fastened the lacey bra. Next, she stepped into the dress. It was sleeveless, hugged her breasts perfectly, landed higher on her thighs than she remembered, and indeed she needed assistance with the zipper.

Damn him for already predicting that fact. She rounded the bed and came to the balcony doorway. "You can zip me now."

He turned around, but she had already put her back to him to avoid his reaction and his expression. Both had been detrimental to her resolve last night. When his hands landed on her lower back to hold the fabric steady while he tugged the zipper, she held her breath.

Why did he have to be so damn…Noah. Smell so good. Look so delectable. His touch instantly heated her skin. A chill ran up her spine. Not because she was cold but because every time he touched her, she felt a jolt of desire.

She squeezed her thighs together, something he probably didn't miss, and held her breath, concentrating on the way he slowly zipped her up. His hands landed on her shoulders when he was done. "You look stunning. As usual. But I need you to know something." He slid his hands down her bare arms and turned her around.

She stared at his shirt, realizing for the first time that he had on a pink tie.

He lifted her chin with one finger. "You're a gorgeous woman. You look hot in anything. If you'd brought baggy sweatpants and loose T-shirts to wear to dinner, you still would have taken my breath away. So, don't worry about how sexy your dresses are. I love them." He slowly lowered his lips to her cheek and kissed her.

She closed her eyes, wishing he had kissed her on the lips. Deep and thoroughly. She was a disaster, constantly sending him mixed messages. She was also receiving mixed messages from her brain, so it wasn't hard to believe they poured off her at the same time.

On instinct, she grabbed his biceps and leaned into him. "I'm sorry. For everything."

He set a hand on her lower back and threaded the other in her hair—the hair she'd worn down tonight because she knew he liked it that way. "Me too." Those words had a dozen meanings, but she decided she didn't want to know what he was thinking.

Every inhale was excruciating. She wanted him so badly it hurt. All day long she had missed him. She didn't want to spend this cruise avoiding him. She wanted to be with him. "I'm such a bitch." She set her chin on his chest and looked up at him. "I had a terrible day. I missed you."

He grinned. "Thank God. I'm glad it wasn't just me. My day was shit without you." His hand threaded in her hair, tugging it slightly to pull her head back farther.

What if she threw in the towel? Tossed common sense out the door and let him in? She was fairly certain that no matter what she did, nothing would change. If she spent the week avoiding him, she would feel awful all the time wishing he were with her. If she spent all her time with him, they might enjoy each other's company too much. Even if she had sex with him, the outcome would still be the same. No matter which route she took.

He brushed a few hairs off her forehead. "What's going on in that deep mind of yours?"

"Weighing my options," she admitted. "Damned if I do. Damned if I don't."

"If the *do* and *don't* are meant to imply that you're contemplating sleeping with me, let me help. I'm not going to have sex with you. I promised I wouldn't, and I won't break that trust. So, how about you relax, put that out of your mind, and let's go have fun. We'll stuff ourselves until we can't breathe and then check out the entertainment."

She liked that idea. She wasn't sure she could let go of her concerns about how her body ignited every time he touched her, but she'd never known him to go back on his word, so it was reasonable to trust him to keep his dick in his pants, so to speak. "Let's do it."

CHAPTER 9

"Wait...what did you say? I misunderstood. I could swear instead of snorkeling, you just said zip-lining. Those are very different words." Ellie tipped her head to one side and tapped her ear against her hand as if she had a gallon of ocean water in her head.

He laughed. "You heard me. You're gonna need close-toed shoes, shorts, and a shirt you don't mind wearing under the harness."

"Harness?" She set her hands on her hips. The ship was supposed to dock in half an hour. They'd gotten up early to prepare to get off. Now she was considering climbing back into bed. "I didn't get this memo."

"I know. I didn't tell you on purpose." He shoved several things into a backpack.

"Why would you do that?" she asked, tapping one foot nervously.

"So that you wouldn't freak out unnecessarily ahead of time like you are now." He grinned that stupid, sexy, lopsided, I-know-you-well grin. Ordinarily, she found it endearing. Right now, it was far from anything resembling endearing.

"So, your plan for the day is to climb up into the trees, hook onto a little rope, and jump? You better hurry and get downstairs so you can find someone willing to join you."

Now he laughed. "You're joining me. It's going to be fun. You'll see."

"No. See, I guess you don't remember every detail about me."

"I remember fine. You don't like heights. I'm clear. But you can do this. It's exhilarating. I heard the views are amazing. You don't want to miss out on this experience."

"Sure I do." She opened the sunscreen and squirted some in her palm. As she rubbed it into her legs, she continued. "You can show me pictures afterward. I'm sure there's a perfectly good beach right at sea level I can sit on while you jump from tall platforms in the sky."

He dropped his backpack, took her shoulders, and held her gaze. "Go with me." His voice was serious. Pleading, but not in an annoying way.

She sighed.

"I promise I'll let you pick the excursion tomorrow. Something at sea level. Zip-lining will be so much fun, but not if you don't go with me."

She blew out another breath and dropped her shoulders. "You've lost your mind this time."

"You'll come?" He sounded so excited. How could

she tell him no?

"I'll come. I won't enjoy it, but I'll come."

"Excellent. We'll see."

Three hours later, Ellie was certain she was going to lose her breakfast. Her nausea was the only thing keeping Noah alive however. If she hadn't been so queasy from standing too far off the ground on a rickety platform, she might have had the energy to push Noah off the top.

His arms came around her from behind. "Deep breaths. Don't look down from the platform. Wait until you're swinging through the trees."

"Oh great. That makes me feel so much better."

He inched her closer to the edge as the last of the people in their group all took their first death jump. There were ten in all. Ellie had paid little attention to any of them. She hadn't paid close attention to Noah either for that matter. She'd been too busy checking and rechecking all the buckles and hooks and latches on her harness while watching closely how each person was attached to the wire above their heads before they jumped.

Jumped wasn't the right word of course. No one was really jumping. This wasn't a bungee cord. But as far as she was concerned, it was just as insane.

Two more people were left before her.

Noah had his hands around her waist, his lips on her ear. "Deep breaths. You can do this."

"How much are we paying for this death-defying experience anyway?"

He chuckled. "Don't worry about it."

She twisted her neck around. "You're not paying for my excursions, Noah. Forget it."

"How about you pay for tomorrow's adventure, then?"

"Let me guess. You arranged for us to go skydiving." She flinched as the words left her mouth, not at all sure he wouldn't have made such a reservation. It was entirely possible.

He laughed again. "Nope. I knew I wouldn't be able to get you to do that. And I've jumped out of plenty of planes. I don't need that experience. But I've never gone zip-lining."

"Good. Let's keep it at sea level tomorrow, or slightly below the water. Minus one is good."

He lifted a brow. "We could go for minus forty. They have one-day certification for scuba diving."

She shook her head. "Not a chance on that either. I'm not fond of being too far above or below the surface of the earth."

He kissed her nose. "Snorkeling it is then."

Suddenly, it was her turn. Noah insisted she go before him out of fear she would chicken out and leave him spending the day alone. His concerns were legit.

Her hands were shaking as she stepped to the edge. The man in charge of this platform smiled broadly at her. "First time?"

"Yes. How many people have fallen to their deaths?" she asked, not joking.

He laughed anyway as if she were hilarious. "Zero." He held up a large carabiner and hooked it above her head. Then he did the same with another one. "This is the safest thing you could be doing right now. I promise. Your chances of being involved in an accident on the ATV tour are far greater. We have had zero accidents on this zip line since it opened."

She nodded, only marginally mollified by his words.

Noah grabbed her hand and gave it a squeeze. "You're going to love it. Just relax."

She shot him a glare, or tried to, and took a deep breath. Two seconds later she was screaming loud enough to disrupt not just the animals but the flora too. And then she sucked in a sharp breath, opened her eyes, and looked around. The air felt strange blowing against her face with so much speed, but it also cooled her heated skin and calmed her nerves slightly.

The view was so unbelievably amazing that she forgot she was gliding over the trees for a moment as she soaked in the beautiful scenery. And then it was over. Her harness jerked on her body as she came to a stop at the next platform. A woman working that station used a long pole to draw her the final few feet.

It was over almost before it began. Probably a good thing since she was fairly certain she'd held her breath the entire time. Her legs were jelly as she stepped onto the platform while the rest of the vacationers in her group all clapped.

She gave them a wan smile and turned around to watch for Noah. He arrived looking cool as a cucumber. She seriously doubted he had screamed bloody murder like she had. Hell, the man was a Navy SEAL. He'd been through things she could never even imagine. Ziplining would be a walk in the park for him.

The second he was disconnected from the first line and attached safely to the platform, he pulled her into his arms. His smile was infectious. His lips were inches from hers. "You're still alive."

"Yeah. Don't gloat."

"Did you love it?"

"Jury is still out." She wasn't kidding. It had been exhilarating but also frightening at the same time. That balance was going to have to tip more toward the fun and less toward the scary before she would call this a good time. "How are you so unfazed?"

He lifted a brow. "Babe, I've done things that would make your skin crawl with far less safety equipment."

She cringed. Of course.

He kissed her gently, melting another piece of her heart. He was slowly chipping away at her resolve not to let herself fall so hard for him that she lost a piece of herself. Her recovery from this vacation was already going to take months. Possibly years.

She was also fully aware she was kidding herself. He'd owned her heart for most of her life. She couldn't give him something he already held in his palm. But the pain of all these memories was going to cut into her like a sharp knife later.

By the time she got to the fourth line, she had to admit she was having fun. She didn't even scream as she stepped off the platform.

Noah was beaming from ear to ear when they were

finished. She was confident his excitement had little to do with how much fun he'd had personally and far more to do with successfully luring her to not only face her fear but conquer it.

He took her hand and threaded their fingers together as they ambled slowly back to the bus, and he didn't release her during the ride or on the walk to the ship either.

A sense of contentment settled over her like the sort someone would feel when their life was tidy and perfect. If she ignored the universe and focused on nothing but this blip in the middle of her stupid existence, she could even agree.

This was paradise. Gorgeous weather. Luxurious vacation. The man of her dreams in her bed. The only thing that would make it even more perfect would be if she could somehow erase history and keep Noah Seager for the rest of her life.

They stopped at the bar next to the pool when they got back on the ship for a drink. Noah ordered for them —his standard red wine, her standard gin and tonic. As he handed her the cold glass, he lifted his in a toast. "To new experiences."

She touched his glass with hers. "To not falling to our deaths."

He chuckled. "I'm far more concerned with getting stung by a jellyfish tomorrow than a fall from the zip line."

He had a point. "Did you have to bring up jellyfish?" she teased. "Great. Now I'm going to lie awake worrying about tentacles."

"Mmm." He took a sip of his wine, a dangerous twinkle in his eye. "I'll do my best to wear you out until you're so exhausted you can't help but sleep."

She shivered and looked away. The promise in his words jerked her pussy to life and made her clench her thighs together.

For the millionth time, she worried he had a singular goal of getting between her legs. He didn't understand that it wasn't that simple. Not for her. Even if she were drunk and totally high on arousal, she would never be able to let her guard down on that issue. Wasn't going to happen.

"Hey." He'd leaned closer to her. "Let's change into our suits and go sit in the hot tub in the adult section. The hot water will soothe your muscles. You're going to be sore tomorrow from the tension."

He was right. Why was he always right? "Good idea." *And why didn't I bring any one-piece suits with me?*

Still sipping their drinks, they returned to their cabin. She changed in the bathroom and found him in swim trunks when she reemerged.

His gaze was on her again. Heated. Intense. "You were the cutest girl in school, but Ellie, you are so much more beautiful now."

"Thank you," she managed to murmur as her face heated. She looked away to slide her feet into her flip-flops, partially to avoid his gaze and partially to keep from staring at his damn chest. Every time he was shirtless, she had the urge to flatten her palms on him and taste every inch of his bronzed skin.

He didn't say anything else, but he held her hand

again as they walked to the front of the ship and made their way to the hot tubs. Luckily not everyone had re-boarded yet, so it wasn't too crowded.

She sighed as she slipped into the water. He was right. Her muscles were tight from the anxiety of the zip line.

He sat on the bench and pulled her between his legs. Moments later, his hands were on her shoulders, massaging the tension.

No one else was in this particular hot tub at the moment, so she let herself relax, closed her eyes, and tried not to moan every time he hit a particularly tight muscle.

His hands were efficient and everywhere. He worked up and down her back until she was putty and feared she might slide under the water and drown.

As if he could read every nuance of her, he eased her back against his chest and wrapped his arms around her under her breasts, holding her like a lover would on their honeymoon.

She leaned her head on his shoulder and sighed for probably the tenth time. "You spoil me."

He kissed the sensitive spot behind her ear, but said nothing.

She let herself enjoy this perfect moment for a long time. Her mind once again straying to the *what ifs*. What if they had spent the last fourteen years together? What if they could stay together now for the rest of their lives?

"Hey…" he whispered. "What's this about?"

She hadn't realized she'd been silently crying until

he wiped a tear from her cheek. How he'd noticed in the steamy water was a mystery.

She swallowed her emotion. "It's nothing. I'm just happy." She forced a smile and met his gaze. Damn, he was handsome. His brow was furrowed in concern, but his strong features and jawline made her reach up to stroke a finger along his lips and then his brow. She wanted to wipe away his concern.

He let his expression relax slightly, holding her gaze for a long time. Finally, someone else slid into the hot tub and broke their cocoon. "We should head back to the room. It's formal night."

"Oh, that's right." She bit her lip, remembering what she'd brought for the occasion. Her belly fluttered with a mix of excitement and concern for how he would react to her dress. She loved the way he so outwardly worshiped her with his gaze, but she also was aware of the fact that she was walking a fine line teasing him. Tempting him with something he could not have.

Noah climbed out first and then reached for her hand to help her. Such a gentleman. Thoughtful. Kind. Considerate. Loving. The perfect match for her.

She shook those thoughts from her mind as he slid her flimsy cover-up over her and tugged it into place. "You do realize these things are the most useless items in your wardrobe, right?"

She grinned. "They add to the mystery."

"That's for sure." He shot her a heated look and then took her hand again to lead her back to their cabin.

CHAPTER 10

Noah hadn't taken his gaze off Ellie for over an hour. He wasn't sure he'd blinked from the moment she put the silver dress on and let him turn around. She had never looked sexier. Not even in any of her plethora of bikinis.

The material was soft and silky. He had no idea what it was, but it clung to her in all the right places, accentuating her breasts, which were encased in a strapless bra tonight. Her cleavage made him drool. The thin straps that held the dress up didn't look sturdy enough to do the job but had somehow managed to keep her from flashing anyone in the dining room so far.

The silver material shined and glistened in the light, sparkling in different places with every move. It reached her ankles, but had a slit up the side that gave everyone a glimpse of her thigh with every step. His hand had itched to run up the slit and between her legs for every one of the sixty minutes since he'd first seen it.

The strappy silver heels she wore pulled it all together. He wasn't ordinarily the sort of man who would notice so many aspects of a woman's clothing, but this was Ellie. He'd always noticed everything about her.

He suspected she wasn't wearing panties again since he saw no discernable evidence, which did nothing to keep his cock from remaining stiff under the table.

She had a twinkle in her eye when she tipped her head to one side and parted her lips. "Tell me we're really going snorkeling tomorrow, and you don't intend to blindside me with some death-defying craziness again."

"We are," he assured her, reaching across to take her hand. He couldn't keep from touching her. Anywhere. All the time.

And she let him, which made his heart race every time also. She had even stopped flinching when he encircled her in his embrace. Progress.

He stroked the back of her hand with his thumb, saying nothing, enjoying the way her face was calmer tonight. The worry she'd carried between her brows for the first few days was lessening. She was starting to trust him, if that made any sense. She had no reason not to trust him. Perhaps she was just getting comfortable in his presence.

Her hair was swept up in the front, a silver clip holding her curls away from her face. She had pointed a finger at him when she stepped out of the bathroom and narrowed her gaze in warning, saying, "Leave the clip alone. It goes with the dress. I left plenty of my hair down in back."

He'd nodded, his tongue caught, unable to speak as she admonished him in a way he wished she would do every night for the rest of their lives. He'd give anything to have that silly conversation every day with her. Him pulling her hair out of the confines of rubber bands and clips. Her swatting at him and complaining about how long it took her to get it just right.

Those were the precious moments he lived for.

Their main course arrived, and he had to release her hand. Renaldo winked at him after he set their plates down as if he knew how deep Noah had fallen for her and suspected his road to heaven was an uphill battle. A wink of encouragement. Renaldo was in tune with all kinds of nuances from his guests.

Their steaks were delicious, and they both intermittently moaned around bites. By the time their desserts were in front of them, Noah was so stuffed, he didn't think he could swallow another bite. He leaned back and watched as Ellie enjoyed her chocolate soufflé, the way she savored every morsel, the flick of her tongue when she reached out to catch a drop on her spoon, her full pink lips now devoid of gloss.

She was gorgeous.

He swallowed over a lump in his throat. She was his. He wouldn't be able to let her go. Not after this vacation. Not ever. Not even for a single day.

There was no way they could part ways when they

got off the ship. He fisted his palms in his lap, hoping she wouldn't notice his anxiety.

She wasn't going to walk away from him. He wouldn't let her. She could fight and claw and scream and yell and stomp her feet all she wanted, but he intended to convince her she was his.

To hell with her fucking secret. She could keep it for all he cared. It would be worth the trade-off. There were no other options.

He pictured them grabbing an Uber together, heading for his parents' house and then hers. Or vice versa. Spending some time with their families. Maybe a few days at each house.

People would be shocked. Too bad. They would get over it.

Karla and Layton would be giddy. That part almost made him cringe. He wasn't looking forward to the satisfaction on their smug faces when they found out they'd gotten what they intended to accomplish.

But first he had to convince the woman across from him.

He also had to prove he could let the past go and never bring it up. It seemed imperative. A fragile agreement. Somehow he knew if he made that promise, he could never break it. He couldn't come to her every few months nagging her to reveal her secret. He would have to swallow it, bury it, and let it go.

It was a huge commitment. To himself. As well as her. And he was ready to make it.

As Ellie set her fork down and leaned back in her chair, she smiled. "It's weird to think of all the experiences you must have had with the navy and then with the SEALs. Like a giant chunk of your life I know nothing about."

A giant chunk she would have known about if she hadn't left me. He cleared his throat. "I was thinking the same thing about you working on Wall Street. I can't picture you rushing around in that environment. How the hell did you end up in that line of work? All you ever wanted to do was teach."

She glanced away and then sighed. When she looked back, her eyes were sad, but she gave him a tiny piece of her. "After we broke up, I needed to reinvent myself, I guess. I wanted to do something totally different. Over the years it turned out I was good at it, and I found myself in New York City. Maybe I needed to prove I could do it. Do anything."

"I can understand that. I'm not surprised either. You *can* do anything. I've always known that about you."

She looked down at her glass, playing with the condensation on the side, fidgeting, avoiding his gaze. She hadn't been entirely honest. There was more to that story, but he wouldn't pressure her.

He would give anything to climb inside her mind and peek around. He also hated that she looked so forlorn now. That hadn't been his intent. He needed to steer this conversation back to something happier. "What's it like standing in that throng of people rushing around the floor of the stock exchange?"

She lifted her gaze, shaking off the melancholy. "It's exhilarating and intense. Makes your heart race. What's it like jumping out of the side of a helicopter into cold water? I assume you've done something like that."

He chuckled. "I have. It's exhilarating and intense. Makes your heart race." Yeah, now they were back on track. He continued, "Most of the guys on my team are also in the process of retiring or getting out. We're all very close. Been through a lot together. I hope we stay in contact as civilians."

"I'm sure you will." Her smile was genuine, and she leaned forward, set her elbow on the table, and put her chin on her palm. "I *know* you will."

After dinner, he led her to the ship's dance club on the upper deck. He needed to feel the sway of her in his arms and get her soft for him before he told her his plan.

The bar was crowded and noisy. It took a few minutes to secure drinks, and then he led her to a booth along the back wall. He didn't let her sit, however. Instead, he took her drink, set it on the table, and tugged her toward the dance floor.

She giggled as he dramatically swept her into his embrace and started swaying to the slow song. Her face lit up. She was happy. In his arms. He made her happy.

He smoothed one palm over her lower back and held her hand between their chests as he looked into her eyes. He wanted to tell her how he felt so badly it hurt, but he held back the words and hoped he conveyed the meaning with his eyes.

He wouldn't risk freaking her out with words of love. The night was too perfect for that. In fact, he vowed to do his best to finish off the evening with her relaxed and content in his arms. His thoughts of the future could wait. The week was only half over. He had three and a half more days to convince her she was his for a lifetime.

When he spotted a man selling roses in the hallway, he excused himself for a moment, left her sipping her drink, and returned with the single white rose.

She looked like she might cry as she took it from him. "You're spoiling me."

"That's the idea."

~

Ellie was admittedly confused as they stepped off the ship the next morning to head for their snorkeling excursion. Yesterday had been prefect. She couldn't imagine anything that could have improved it.

Their evening had been out of a fairy tale, complete with delicious food, dancing, and then standing on their balcony staring at the stars.

Noah had touched her constantly, but he'd never pushed her for anything more. He held her hand or palmed the small of her back. He kissed her neck and stroked the sensitive skin of her shoulders.

When they got back to the room, she'd taken off her heels and joined him on the balcony where he'd pinned her to the railing with his arms and just breathed next to her cheek.

He never said a word about sex or made a move to lure her into anything that would make her uncomfortable. When she went into the bathroom to change into a tank top and shorts, she returned to find him sitting in bed, chest bare, iPad in his hand.

He'd pulled the covers back to let her in, but then set one of his large hands on her thigh and continued to read from his device.

Her body had been heated and tight to the point of explosion, needing more from him and knowing she couldn't ask for it without sounding capricious. So, she'd taken what he offered, curled onto her side against him, set her face on his lap under his iPad, and fallen asleep to the feel of his pulse against her cheek.

Now, they were once again headed to shore for the day.

Noah pointed out a man holding a sign for their tour, and she exhaled in relief to find he hadn't tricked her into something more daring than snorkeling.

As they waited for the rest of the group to arrive, he leaned against the railing on the dock and pulled her between his legs. She leaned back against him and enjoyed the way he smoothed his hands up and down her arms.

Chills covered her skin.

"You cold, baby?" he asked.

"Nope." There weren't words to describe why she had goose bumps. Her mind was still mulling over their odd exchange in the room fifteen minutes ago when she'd declared she was ready to go and reached for the handle on the cabin door to step into the hall.

Noah had grabbed her wrist, hauled her backward, and plucked a pair of white shorts from her drawer. "Woman, I swear to God, you're not wandering around all day in nothing but a bikini and that excuse for a cover-up."

"We're going to the beach and then snorkeling," she informed him, biting the inside of her cheek.

"And between here and there, I'll be batting men off you. Do this for me." He shook the shorts out in front of her. "You can take them off when we get in the water."

She fought the giggle that wanted to erupt out of her throat and instead gave him a fake eye roll, a cocked hip, and pursed lips. She jerked the shorts out of his hand, shrugged them up her legs and hips, buttoned them over her yellow bikini bottoms, and then put her hands on her hips. "Happy?"

Glancing down, she realized she looked far more ridiculous than before, so she pulled the matching yellow cover-up over her head and stuffed it in her bag. "Now can we go?" She knew she was playing with fire. Why on earth she chose to goad him like that was beyond her, but she couldn't help herself.

Noah groaned as predicted, reached back into her drawer, and tugged out a pale green tank top. "Jesus, Ellie. You're killing me."

She smiled, her entire body warming as she pulled the shirt over her head. "*Now* are you happy?" she whined, though she doubted he bought her fake tone.

He smirked, hauled her into his arms, and kissed her lips. "Not really. But it'll do."

"Since when are you so possessive?" she asked as they left the room, him carrying her bag stuffed with everything they might need during the day.

"Since we met sophomore year of high school. Have you forgotten?"

She had not. Not for a minute. His jealousy had been one of the cutest things about him. He never had wanted to share her skin with other guys. Not then and apparently still not today. He never went overboard. Never crossed the line ordering her around about her clothes.

She'd seen him glancing around at others on the lido deck while she sunbathed. She'd also seen him smile when he caught men giving her a double take at dinner and out at night. He was a combination of proud to be seen with her while just possessive enough of her to give a warning glare to anyone who looked too long or stepped too close.

The dynamic between them had always included this low-level subtle dominance from him. Nothing had changed in that area. And it just felt good when he got all macho protective of her. As if she belonged to him.

She did. In theory. She would never belong to another man, that was for sure. But she also wasn't his. Not for the long haul. Just for three more short days.

A van pulled up while she was still enjoying his hands as they smoothed up and down her bare arms. She hated breaking their connection to climb inside.

Twenty minutes later they were on a private beach with an open bar and all the snorkeling gear they desired.

As soon as the mad rush of people claimed their gear and hurried toward the water's edge, she and Noah stepped up. By silent mutual agreement, they'd hung back, letting others go first. She loved that about him, the fact that they were on the same page without words.

By the time they stepped into the warm sand and claimed a pair of lounge chairs, nearly everyone in their group was already swimming out to find the perfect fish.

Ellie tugged off her shirt and shrugged out of her shorts, feeling the heat of Noah's gaze on her skin. She couldn't form words as he opened the sunscreen and began to rub it into her back while she gathered her hair into a messy bun.

His hands moved reverently over her skin. Something in him had changed gradually over the last twenty-four hours. Resigned? Or did he think he'd won some battle? That last thought scared her.

When his hands ran over her shoulders and smoothed the lotion into her chest and even under the edge of the cups of her bikini, she didn't stop him. She watched as her nipples pebbled. There would be no hiding her reaction. However, no one would be able to see what was happening between her legs.

He handed her the lotion next and turned around. She took her time working it into his skin. He'd gotten darker in the last three days. She paid close attention to his trident tattoo and then glanced down at the one peeking out of the top of his swim trunks. She had yet to see that one.

As she worked her way down his back, she took a chance and let the tips of her fingers dip into the waistband of his shorts, nudging them subtly downward, hoping to catch a better look at that nearly hidden tattoo.

Suddenly, his hand reached around and flattened on hers, stopping her before she'd seen the object of her intent. He pressed her palm into his hip and turned around. His gaze was intent, and he gave his head a quick shake. "Don't."

She swallowed her surprised. "Don't what?"

He ignored her, put the lotion away, and grabbed their snorkeling gear. When he finally looked at her again, he was wearing a forced smile. "Ready?" He grabbed her hand with his free one and dragged her toward the water's edge.

"Noah?" she asked, more than curious about his behavior.

When they were knee-deep in water, he handed her a set of fins and a mask and snorkel set. He glanced at her face, his brows still drawn together. "Let it go, Ellie. Please."

She nodded slowly. It was important to him. But now she was more curious than ever. He hadn't mentioned the tattoo a single time, nor had he ever had his shorts down with his back to her for her to see it.

Oh, he'd stood gloriously naked before her. She wouldn't forget that, but he'd put his briefs on before turning around, blocking that tattoo.

She let it go. After all, it would be hypocritical to do otherwise, considering she had her own secrets that were buried deep. His were visible. Hers were in her chest, clenching her heart.

As she strode farther toward the waves next to him,

she adjusted her mask and thought for the first time about what would happen if she bared her soul and spilled the details of that spring with him.

What would he say? How would he react? Bile rose in her throat. She could never do it. She knew him well enough even then to know it would destroy him to know the facts. She'd made choices without including him. Life-altering decisions. He would hate her and be devastated. It would be worse than leaving him in the dark, confused and pissed for the next seventy years.

No. She couldn't do it. Wouldn't take that risk.

She'd been so deep in thought that she hadn't realized they'd stopped. Noah was staring at her, water lapping at his chest and forcing them both to bob up and down with the tide. His expression was again serious. He took her hand. "I'll show you someday, but not today."

The tattoo. He thought she was still freaking out over the tattoo. "Okay." Her voice was breathy.

He leaned in, kissed her forehead, and nodded toward the waves. "Let's go. The fish are waiting."

CHAPTER 11

The sun was warm on Noah's chest as they lay on the lounge chairs on the beach that afternoon. This excursion was laid-back. Snorkeling and eating and drinking leisurely. It was all-inclusive and very relaxing.

Ellie was on her stomach, her face toward him, a slight smile on her lips. Her damn suit was untied so that she wouldn't get a line from the sun, though he had to restrain himself from arguing about it.

He vowed to buy her a house in the suburbs with a secluded pool so she could sunbathe all she wanted in as little clothing as her heart desired with no threat of anyone seeing his woman naked in their yard.

He realized he was staring at her while he conjured that elaborate picture in his mind. A dream. A pipe dream most likely. Though he was making headway. Or so he thought.

She broke their stare-off to reach down and grab her

frozen drink from the little table between them and take a sip.

He picked up his matching one and did the same. It wasn't red wine, but it was better than beer. He'd never really developed a taste for beer, and the beach resort they were at for the day didn't have wine.

She giggled, a sound he adored more than red wine. "How's your drink?"

"It's okay." He made a face. "A little sweet, but refreshing in this heat."

"It is a bit sweet. I promise you we'll return to civilization later this afternoon and find you some dry red elixir."

With her chest lifted up a few inches to take a drink, he could almost see her nipples which made his dick harder and his chauvinistic tendency come to the surface. "That's fine. In the meantime, how about you let me retie your barely existent top."

She giggled, shaking her head, and lay her cheek back on the towel pillow she'd made. "Don't be ridiculous. I'm fine."

He sighed. He would never win that battle in his lifetime. "Did you look at the lineup of possible excursions for tomorrow?"

"No. But I was thinking maybe we could take it easy, sleep late, leisurely leave the ship midday, do some sightseeing, shopping, stuff like that. What do you think?"

"I like it." He smiled. For Ellie, he would do anything. Even shop. He wouldn't do that for any other woman, including his mother.

She closed her eyes, looking content and happy. He loved that look on her, but their days were numbered. At some point he would need to bite the bullet and rock the boat. Even if it capsized.

∾

"Damn, they have a lot of silver stores," Ellie stated after lunch the next day. They were wandering through the tourist shops at the pier, stopping in random stores for souvenirs. She'd grabbed a few postcards and a tank top.

"Want to go in one?" he asked, nodding toward one of dozens of jewelry stores.

"Sure." She couldn't think of anything she might buy, but it was always fun to look.

They wandered around for a few minutes and then came back together at the door. In the next store, Noah picked up a white flowy sundress from a rack. "This would look amazing on you with your new tan."

She smiled. He was right. It was her style.

"Try it on," he insisted.

"Okay." She took it from him, wondering why he was being so insistent, and headed for the fitting room. Maybe he wanted to see it on her. As soon as she had it on, she opened the curtain and peeked out, but she didn't find him.

His loss. She took the dress off, put her shorts and tank top back on, and found him at the cash register.

"Did it fit?" he asked.

"Yep."

"Good. I'm getting it for you." He took it out of her hand and handed it to the cashier.

"You don't have to do that."

"I want to. I'm the one who suggested it. And besides, I'm the one who's going to enjoy looking at it too." He handed the cashier his credit card.

Ellie chewed on her bottom lip, wondering when he thought he was going to see that dress on her. They had one more full day at sea. One day. Two nights. That was it. Her mouth went dry at the thought.

As they stepped outside, he took her hand. "So far on this trip I've spent almost nothing. One excursion and now this dress. I haven't even given Layton a check for the room. I meant to do that when we arrived."

She cringed and glanced up at him. "Layton didn't pay for the room."

"Well, Karla then. Whatever."

"She didn't either."

He stopped walking. "*You* paid for the room?"

"Yeah. Karla arranged it, but I gave her my credit card number. I make way more money than her. She was going to cover the on-board expenses. In her fake world."

"Well, I owe you a lot of money then. Why didn't you let me cover the snorkeling?"

"Because I didn't want to. It's done. I paid for the room weeks ago. It's no big deal."

He frowned at her. *Here we go.*

"You are not covering my half of the room, Ellie. Forget it."

She sighed. "You haven't changed."

"If by that you mean that I'm still a gentleman who pays for my dates when I take them out, then you're right. I haven't changed." He started walking again. He was holding her hand, but kind of tight.

She jerked to free herself, but he didn't let go. "Noah. Stop. Be reasonable. You didn't take me out on a date this time. You got tricked. And besides, you're not even getting sex out of the deal. If you'd met up with Layton instead of being duped into spending the week with me, you'd at least have found a woman on board who was willing to sleep with you."

The moment the words left her lips, she knew she'd stepped in it.

Noah stopped walking again. He pulled her a few feet into an alley between two shops and plastered her against the wall. With one hand on the brick next to her head and the other trapping her at her side, he looked like flames might come out of his ears.

"I didn't mean that the way it sounded."

"Yeah? How did you mean it? Because it sounded to me like you think I've been picking up women at every port for the last decade, fucking them, and leaving them."

"I didn't say that." She kinda did.

"Did I ever once in all the time we were going together give you the impression that you owed me sex or even a trip to first base when I took you out on a date?"

"No." He hadn't. She bit her lower lip again. She felt awful. "I'm sorry."

He stared at her. Hard. "I had intended to share that

room with Layton. It's not a college dorm. I'm not eighteen years old. I wouldn't have brought women back to the room and stuck a sock on the door."

"Of course not." Yeah, she had said some pretty stupid things in her life, but this one topped the list.

He searched her face for a minute.

She licked her dry lips and set her hands on his chest. "I really am sorry. It was stupid and uncalled for."

He closed his eyes, took several deep breaths, and then set his forehead against hers. "Ellie..." Whatever he'd thought to say, he swallowed it back. Instead, he straightened, took her hand, and continued down the sidewalk.

She tried to slow her racing heart as they made their way back to the ship.

"I need a nap," he mumbled as they boarded.

"Okay," she whispered, not even sure if he heard her.

When they got to the room, he dropped their bags and dramatically collapsed onto his back, spread across most of the mattress.

"You want me to go find something to do so you can rest?" she asked tentatively.

He shook his head and reached out a hand. "No. I want you to snuggle into my side and nap with me. I'll sleep better if you're in my arms."

She finally blew out the breath she'd been mostly holding for the last half hour and climbed onto the bed, kicking off her sandals. She curled into his side, set her cheek on his chest, and laid her palm on his abs.

He wrapped his huge arm around her and gave a

squeeze before kissing the top of her head. "Sorry I snapped at you," he said.

"It was my fault. I'm sorry I said such stupid things."

He squeezed her again and then relaxed. In a few minutes, she knew he was asleep, and she enjoyed every moment of his resting body until she succumbed to sleep herself.

CHAPTER 12

As soon as Ellie stepped out of the bathroom that night, her usual towel wrapped around her, she found Noah standing in the cabin, fully dressed for dinner as always, holding a single white rose.

He was smiling at her as he came toward her, and then he trailed the soft petals down her cheek. It was the most romantic gesture of her life. Even after she'd totally pissed him off that afternoon, he'd let it go and proved it was over with the effort.

She tipped her cheek into his hand and then took the rose from him to sniff the fragrant bud. "You sure know how to make a woman feel loved." The words slipped out unbidden. Not that she was wrong. But she probably could have chosen better.

"That's the idea." He smiled warmly at her and set the rose on the bed. "What's the color scheme for tonight? I didn't select my tie yet."

She'd never met a more thoughtful man in her life.

He loved her so totally. She knew it. And he was working his ass off to prove himself worthy. The problem was nothing he could do would erase the past, and she knew he could never let it die.

Nor could she.

They were at an impasse. No amount of roses or fine dining or dancing or kissing could fix this mess. She shoved the distressing thoughts to the back of her mind and turned toward the closet. "The white one we just bought? Or this black one?" She fingered the standard little black dress that no woman would leave home without. "I also have a skirt and blouse I haven't worn yet."

"Wear the white one. I didn't get to see it."

"I stuck my head out to show you, but you were nowhere in sight."

He frowned. "Guess I wandered outside for a moment." He reached for their bags on the floor and pulled it out. "Will it be too wrinkly?" he asked.

"Nope. It's meant to look wrinkled. It's fine." She selected a white lace bra and panty set and lifted her gaze.

"Yeah, yeah, yeah. I'll be on the balcony." He left her there, but this time a knot in her belly tightened. It felt wrong. They were so close and yet so far apart. She longed for more. She wanted to bridge that gap. But she couldn't.

She was still shaking when she was finished dressing. The material of the dress was thin enough that he would see the lace of her bra through the front. The matching thong made her feel sexy. The hem hung at mid-thigh. She decided to put on silver sandals and then turned around and put the silver clip in her hair too.

When she stepped out onto the balcony, Noah turned around. He chuckled. "Damn. I didn't make a very good choice, did I?"

She frowned. "What do you mean?" She glanced down, thinking it fit her nicely and had the perfect combination of flirty and sexy. It was youthful.

"There's nothing for me to zip or tie. I have no reason to put my hands on you."

She giggled and then leaned into him, flattening her palms on his chest. "You don't need a reason. You haven't needed a reason this entire week. I'm not sure you've gone more than a few minutes without touching me since we found each other at the bar."

He smiled. "Fair point."

After selecting a black tie, he grabbed their keycards like every night and stuffed them in his pocket. His hand was on the small of her back as he led her down the hallway.

Unexplained nerves climbed up her spine as they took their seats in the dining room. She had no idea why. Nothing had changed. Except something had. She just couldn't put her finger on it.

Renaldo set a glass of red wine and a gin and tonic in front of them. He was amazing.

Every course of their meal was delicious as always, though Noah seemed quieter than usual. She wanted to ask if something was on his mind, but she couldn't bring herself to say a word and rock their precarious boat.

When the dessert plates were cleared away, Noah set his wine on the table and met her gaze. "I got you something."

She tipped her head to one side. "What?"

He reached into his pocket and pulled out a navy velour pouch. After a moment's hesitation, he slid it across the table. He looked incredibly nervous, which also explained why he'd been a little off for the entire evening.

She was nervous too. "Noah?"

"Open it." He forced a smile. "It won't bite."

She reached with tentative fingers to pick up the pouch, opened the gold drawstring, and tipped it over. A silver chain fell into her palm. When she set the pouch down, she realized there was a pendant.

A single rose.

It was so beautiful.

Tears welled up in her eyes. Her hands were shaking.

Noah leaned across the table and wrapped both her hands in his. "Be mine, Ellie. Please. Say you'll give us a chance. Don't walk away from this." He didn't wait for a response. Instead, he stood from the table, rounded it, and took the necklace from her hand.

He straightened it out, brushed her hair to one side, and fastened it at her neck.

She couldn't speak. She fingered the tiny rose against her chest and closed her eyes. She couldn't have been more emotional if he'd given her a diamond ring. Did he realize how much more this meant to her?

He crouched next to her and tipped her head his direction with a finger under her chin. "Don't cry, baby. It was supposed to make you happy."

A tear fell, and then another.

He stood, took her hand, and helped her rise. With an arm around her shoulders, he led her from the dining room and down the hall. He didn't take her to a club or a show or a bar. He took her back to their cabin and shut the door.

When they were finally alone, he cupped her face and kissed her gently. "Be mine, Ellie," he repeated. "I don't care about the past. It's over. I want you with me every day for the rest of my life."

More tears. Of joy and sadness combined. She wiped them with her hand. He leaned toward the desk and grabbed her a tissue, pressing it into her palm. And then he wrapped her in his arms and rocked them both back and forth in the dim light of the room.

One hand threaded into her hair, the other one flat on her lower back. "I love you so much, baby. I won't accept no for an answer because I know you love me too. Don't let this end here."

She tipped her head back. "Love isn't the problem, Noah. I never stopped loving you."

He swallowed visibly. "Don't say *no*. Think about it. Please."

She set her cheek against his chest again, uncertain how to respond to him. He'd asked her to think about it. So, at least she didn't need to shoot him down this second.

"Come on. Let's go out onto the balcony. It's so nice outside."

She let him lead her through the sliding door. Instead of sitting, he pressed her against the balcony and settled his hands on the railing, trapping her as he'd done several times before. It made her heart race. Being surrounded by him always did.

He set his chin on her shoulder lightly, and they both stared out into the night. "There are so many stars out here."

"Yeah. It's beautiful." She covered his hands with hers on the railing.

After a few minutes, he turned his lips toward her neck and kissed her behind the ear. He didn't stop, however. Instead, he nibbled a path to her shoulder and then up toward her mouth.

She tipped her head to give him better access, needing this kiss more than her next breath. She needed all of him. It was a stabbing pain in her chest.

When his tongue stroked her lips and then dipped inside, she turned around to face him, grabbing his waist and letting him deepen the kiss further.

Suddenly, she felt a desperation born of pent-up sexual frustration and days of denial. Years of denial. She couldn't have sex with him. She wouldn't. But she could do everything else. And she wanted to more than anything in the world. She wanted to bring him pleasure.

His hands slid to her back and then down to cup her ass. He moaned into her mouth, tipping the other direction as if he could kiss her deeper if his head were angled just right.

She shoved him backward so that they made their way back into the cabin. It only took a few steps for him to hit the bed. And then he was falling, taking her with him, not breaking the kiss as she came down on top of him.

The lighting was dim, but he reached back with one hand and flipped it off, leaving them bathed in nothing but the moon and the stars. She reached for his shirt and tugged it out of his dress pants. Her hands went to his tie next, but she couldn't get it loose.

Straddling his waist, she worked on the buttons instead while Noah reached between them to tug off his tie. After fumbling around like a randy teenager, she had his chest bare and yanked her lips from his to explore the expanse of flesh she'd been staring at all week.

She was out of her mind. This was a bad idea. But she couldn't stop. She needed to taste him. All of him. She wouldn't take him in her pussy, but she wanted every inch of him in her mouth.

When she kissed her way down to his belt, he cupped her head. "Baby…"

She batted his hands away and worked his belt buckle, and then the button and zipper on his pants.

"Ellie… Baby…" He clasped her shoulders and tried to tug her up his body.

She lifted her gaze. "Please. Noah, let me do this."

He stared into her eyes for a long time, reading her.

Finally, he licked his lips. "I won't enter your pussy until you agree to be mine. It would kill me otherwise."

"Good. Because I'm going to take you in my mouth."

He swallowed hard, his eyes narrowed now, his expression one of concern. "I…"

"I want to, Noah. Give me this."

He nodded slowly and released her, relaxing more fully onto the bed as she wiggled down his body and then worked his pants over his hips and lower. She had to stand to take off his shoes and socks, and then she tugged his pants the rest of the way down. His briefs went next.

For a moment she stared at his impressive length. She hadn't had a chance to get up close and personal with it this week. It was time to make that happen. His erection bobbed against his abs, pleading with her. It was thick and hard, and a drop of come already leaked from the tip.

His voice was gravelly when he spoke. "Take off your dress. I want to see you in that lacey bra and panties."

Before she climbed back onto the bed, she pulled the dress over her head.

"You are so fucking sexy." He reached for her.

She smoothed her hands up his thighs and crawled between his legs.

Slowly, as if they had all the time in the world, she licked a line up his cock from base to head.

He moaned, his hands landing on her hair, threading into it but not pressuring her. She enjoyed the feel of his strength as she sucked the tip into her mouth and then swirled her tongue around the head and through the slit.

"Jesus." That one word came out on a breath.

She sucked him deeper next, sliding her tongue along the vein. He was bigger than she remembered. Not that she'd given him hundreds of blowjobs in high school. But she had a few times. And he was definitely larger.

Everything about him was larger.

She also hadn't given a blowjob since the last time she'd held him in her mouth fourteen years ago, so she was nervous.

He didn't seem to mind or notice her lack of experience. Considering the last time she'd done this, she was certain she had fumbled and made a mess of it.

She smoothed her hands up his thighs and cupped his scrotum, gently rolling the skin there until he stiffened and bucked his cock deeper from beneath her.

He was panting when he set his hips back down. "Ellie…"

She loved the way he said her name. She loved the way he said every word when he was aroused. It empowered her to continue. It also made her wet. Her panties were soaked.

Noah's hands trailed lower to her breasts, but he could only reach the upper swell, so he dipped his fingers into the lace of her bra to flick over her nipples.

She squirmed, her arousal shooting through the roof at the contact. It went straight to her sex and left her panting around his girth. She also sucked him deeper and let her cheeks hollow.

He groaned. "Baby... I'm gonna come."

That's the idea.

"You're too good at that. It's been so long... I need..." His voice trailed off, and she forced her throat to open so she could take him deeper. She wrapped one hand around the base of his cock and sucked him harder and faster, lifting up and down rapidly until he let go of her entirely, gripped the bedding at his sides, and stiffened. His entire body went tight. A glance at his face showed his mouth open and his eyes closed.

On the next pass, he jerked, his body thrusting upward again as his seed shot into the back of her mouth. It was the most beautiful thing to watch. This giant of a man, a Navy SEAL no less, losing all control. For her.

For her.

For her.

She sucked him until he was completely spent and flinched slightly. When she finally released him with a light pop, she continued kissing his abs, working her way up to his chest, and then flicking her tongue over a nipple.

He made a primal growl, grabbed her biceps, and flipped her onto her back.

She squealed at the sudden change.

His mouth came over hers so fast she didn't have a chance to catch her breath. He kissed her like a man desperate to stake his claim. His hands landed on her waist and trailed up to her breasts. He cupped them and squeezed hard enough for a jolt of pain combined with intense pleasure to make her writhe.

His knee landed between her legs, and he released her lips to dip his head and suck her breast, lace and all.

A hand wiggled under her back, and seconds later, her bra was freed, and his mouth was suckling her nipple deep and hard.

"Noah…" Her turn to breathe out his name.

She was completely relaxed, knowing he'd meant what he'd said and he wouldn't enter her with his cock. It was all the promise she needed. But she was on fire for him, and she lifted her pussy to rub against his thigh.

He lowered one hand to her hip and pressed her firmly against the mattress, her breast popping out of his mouth so he could meet her gaze. "Stay still. Let me."

The tone of his voice shot her arousal up ten notches, and she bit her lip as she nodded.

He smiled. "God, I love you. I love everything about you. I love the way you moan and squirm and writhe beneath me. I even love the way you bite your lip when you're trying not to cry out." He cupped her breasts reverently, kissed the tips gently, and then slid down the bed.

His hands were on her panties in a heartbeat, and then her thong was over her hips and off her body just as quickly. Without warning, he grabbed her thighs, spread them open, and lowered his mouth to her sex.

She cried out, just as he'd predicted, the bite on her lip no longer effective under the onslaught of his lips and tongue. When he sucked her clit into his mouth, her vision blurred. She tipped her head back and concentrated on every single detail. Every sensation. Every stroke of his tongue over her sensitive flesh.

His thumbs slid up her thighs and between her legs to part her lower lips and then he dipped one inside her. Her body gripped him instinctively.

She bucked, but he held her steady with his other hand on her belly. Between the flicking of his tongue and the sucking of his lips and the thrusting of his thumb, she was losing her grasp on reality.

She was going to come. She never came this fast. Not even with batteries. But then again nothing electronic in her apartment compared to the multifaceted assault coming from this man she dearly loved more than life itself.

He pulled out his thumb and replaced it with a finger, thrusting deeper. She arched her chest since she couldn't lift her hips. Her breasts felt heavy. Her hands roamed his shoulders until she couldn't control them anymore and gripped him so hard she would probably leave an indentation from her nails.

The suction increased. The flicking faster. And then he hit the sweet spot in her pussy, angling his finger so that he stroked over it rapidly. That was it. She couldn't hold back another moment. She was already falling, her entire body pulsing with the ripples of her arousal as both her clit and her channel seemed to participate.

The orgasm lasted longer than any she remembered. And then she was panting as he eased slowly off her sensitive nub and nibbled around it in a circle. Worshiping her.

He pulled his finger out last, his gaze on her. "That

was so beautiful, baby. I could do that to you every night of my life."

She tried to smile, but her face wasn't registering messages from her brain yet.

Flattening his hand on her belly, he climbed up her body and settled on one hip along her side, his head in the palm of his hand. "You're tighter now than you were in high school. How the hell do you manage that? I thought I wouldn't be able to get my finger back out." His voice was teasing as he leaned down to kiss her neck.

When he lifted his face to catch her gaze again, his free hand trailing up from her waist to gently toy with her breast, he suddenly paused. Frozen.

Dammit.

"Ellie…"

She looked away, not wanting to have this conversation. Ever. But here it was. He wasn't the sort of guy who would let something like this go. Not a chance.

"My God, Ellie." His voice was softer. Lower. He released her breast to grasp her chin and turn her face toward him. "Please tell my you've had sex with other men."

Her face heated, but he wouldn't be able to see it in the dim lighting. Besides, she was already flushed from the orgasm. She blinked at him and bit her lip again.

He groaned. "Baby, why?"

Don't cry. Don't cry. God, don't cry.

There was no way to hold back the tears, however.

His expression was impossible to read as he wiped

the tears away and then traced the edge of her lips. "Baby. Jesus. I—"

She shook her head. "Please. Don't say anything. Please."

He swallowed hard and nodded. "Okay." He lowered his head to her shoulder and held her close. "Okay. It's okay. It's going to be okay." He stroked her face and kissed her neck and continued to whisper. "I love you so much. Baby, you have no idea." His voice trailed off.

Thank God he stopped talking. He kept touching her. Everywhere. But he didn't speak or force her to look at him.

She gradually relaxed in his arms. At some point he pulled the covers back and managed to get them under the soft blankets. And then he hauled her into his arms and didn't let her go.

It took her a while to let sleep drag her under, but eventually it did, and she slept better than she'd slept in years.

CHAPTER 13

Sun was streaming into the room when Ellie woke up. Noah's hand was on her belly, but he was flat on his stomach, his face relaxed in sleep. She watched him for several minutes, memorizing everything about him, and then she slid out from under his hand, careful not to wake him.

She padded to the bathroom, quietly closed the door, used the toilet, and came back out. As she stepped closer, thinking to grab a pair of panties and a tank top, she stopped dead.

The sheets had worked their way down Noah's body. His leg was out and so was his right hip. She blinked several times as she leaned over him and then gasped.

A single rose. Intricate. The stem reaching down his butt. It must have hurt. If she wasn't mistaken, her initials were woven into the stem too. Yep. EG. Not a doubt.

She stumbled backward, unable to stop herself, and

fell against the closet so hard it banged shut. Apparently, it hadn't been fully closed.

Noah jerked awake, his head lifting and turning her direction. He shook himself out of the sleepy fog. "Ellie? You okay?" He slowly pushed his chest off the bed.

Her gaze was on his ass, though, and she shook her head. "No. Not even a little."

He lowered his eyes to the spot she was staring at and came completely off the bed. "Shit." Instantly, he was in her face. "Don't freak out."

She was so far past that. "Don't freak out? Are you serious? You have me tattooed to your ass, Noah."

"It's just a rose." He ran a hand through his tousled hair but didn't touch her.

"It's way more than a rose, and you know it." Her voice was high-pitched, squeaking.

He set one hand on the closet next to her head. "It's a rose."

"My fucking initials are woven into the stem, Noah," she shouted.

He sighed. "Yes. They are."

"That's…creepy."

He shoved off the closet. "Why? Why is it so fucking creepy that I put a small rose on my hip as a symbol of the only woman I've ever loved."

She flinched, wrapped her arms around her naked chest, and took a step away from him. Her head was shaking. "You can't love me."

"Why the fuck not?" He was also yelling now.

"Because I hurt you," she retorted. "I hurt you so

badly I messed you up. You can't love me. You need to let me go."

He lurched forward, apparently done giving her distance, and grabbed her biceps. "I'm not fucking letting you go. Not now. Not ever. If you run from me, I will find you. You're mine. You've always been mine. I don't care what happened fourteen years ago. I never should have let you go then. I should have hunted you down and dragged your ass back home. I was a fool. I made a mistake. I won't do it again. This time you're mine."

She was shaking now. Her voice trembled as she addressed him. "You can't have me. I'm not available."

He glanced down at her body. "You haven't even fucked another man in fourteen years, Ellie. How the hell do you figure you're not still mine and always have been?"

She shook her head violently again. "Because I'm not going to fuck you now. Or ever. So you have to let me go." How had she let things get this far? She was so stupid. Weak.

His entire body jerked. He still held her biceps. His eyes narrowed. His nostrils flared. He was angrier than she'd ever seen him, and she oddly sensed it wasn't at her. "Did someone touch you?"

Her eyes widened.

"You were raped, weren't you? Someone fucking put their hands on you in that last week before graduation."

"What?" She was shaking so badly she thought she might collapse, but he held her up, pressing her into the closet and using his hips to steady her torso. They were both naked. It didn't matter. It dawned on her how he might assume she'd been raped. She had to set him straight. "No."

He was shaking. A moment ago, he'd looked like he might kill someone. Now he was going to do it slowly, ripping them limb from limb.

"Noah," she screamed to get his attention. "No one touched me. I was not raped."

He didn't believe her. He stared at her, his brows furrowed. Fury came off him in waves. His gaze darted back and forth between her eyes.

She lowered her voice several octaves and set her hands on his hips. "No one has ever touched me besides you. I swear."

Moments passed as she waited for her words to sink in. His breathing slowed. His eyes softened marginally. He loosened his grip on her biceps. "Then what, baby? Tell me right now. What the hell happened?"

She closed her eyes and leaned her forehead against his chest, drawing in a lungful of air, knowing that her life was about to take a turn she'd never wanted to witness.

He pulled her into his arms, cradling her closer, stroking his hands up and down her back in a soothing gesture she did not deserve. His chin rested on the top of her head. And he waited.

After the words left her mouth, she would never be able to take them back. He would hate her. She would never see that love on his face again.

It was so overwhelming that she couldn't stop the tears from falling even before she admitted what she'd done. She gripped his back. "I'm so sorry. I didn't know what to do. I was scared. I was so alone. You had the navy. You had your whole life in front of you." She was sobbing now, gut-wrenching sobs that shook her entire frame.

He tipped her head back, forcing her to meet his gaze. He was calmer now. In pain, but a different pain. The pain was for her this time. Because he didn't know yet. "Tell me, baby. Whatever it is, we'll get through it."

They wouldn't. She knew they couldn't. But she had no choice now. "I got pregnant."

He flinched, but he didn't release her gaze. He licked his lips. "You... But we used protection. Every time."

She stared at him. "I know. But it happened anyway. A condom must have broken. I don't know what happened."

A million emotions crossed his face, one after another: worry, anger, relief, concern, and then his expression settled on betrayal. "So, you just... You decided to leave me instead of telling me?"

She nodded. "I thought it was best. You'd talked about joining the navy and becoming a SEAL for as long as I'd known you." She rushed to continue. To explain the unexplainable. The horror of keeping this from him. "I knew you wouldn't go if you knew. You had everything all planned out. Navy, SEALs, marriage, kids. In that order. You talked about it all the time. You deserved that tidy package. You deserved to head for the navy and find another woman who could fulfill that dream. I didn't want to ruin your life because of some broken condom. It wasn't fair."

He was still processing as she rambled. "Let me get this straight. You broke up with me, pregnant with my baby, and left home to have an abortion?"

Her eyes shot wide. "No." She shook her head. "No," she repeated. "I never considered an abortion for a single moment. I wouldn't do that. I couldn't."

His eyes were wild, darting around the room and landing on her face. "Where is the baby now? Did you give it up for adoption?"

She shook her head again. She was totally fucking this up. As she'd known she would if she ever had to tell him. "I had a miscarriage. At eleven weeks." She let her face drop to the floor, the power of those words coming from her mouth for the first time in her life, draining her.

She was consumed with grief for their unborn child even now. Perhaps more than she had been at the time. The words were out there, floating around the room. Sucking up the oxygen. Her knees buckled as she started crying so hard she couldn't stand any longer or see anything.

Noah let her slide to the floor. He lowered to sit on the bed in front of her. He was no longer touching her.

She sobbed. Ugly sobs that came from deep in her soul. Pain she had repressed for fourteen years, never allowing it to come fully out because it hurt too bad to face it.

When she couldn't bear to cry in front of him any longer, she found the strength to crawl to the bathroom a few feet away, shut herself inside, and sit on the floor of the cramped space with her back against the door.

Tears continued to stream down her face, but she was no longer sobbing out of control. She leaned her forehead against her knees, drawing them up tight, her arms wrapped around her shins.

She cried for the child she'd lost and the man she'd hurt. She cried for the years she'd held back her grief. She cried for the wasted lives, ruined by her choices.

She'd been so young. So afraid. So alone. She couldn't tell him. It would have ruined his life. He would have stayed with her, given up his dreams, and resented her for the rest of both their lives.

In the end, her grief undoubtedly killed their child. Her stupidity and pigheadedness. She'd taken her entire savings and left home, driven to a campsite where she'd gone several times with her family in her childhood. A place she'd known she could rent a cabin with cash and take some time to think.

She figured she'd been nine weeks pregnant when she left.

She'd known Noah had gone to boot camp a week after she took off. She hadn't had a plan. She'd spent most of her time crying and lying on the small cot in the room. She hadn't eaten enough. She'd had no appetite. Before she could pull herself together and figure out what to do, it had been over.

Remembering that day made her cry harder again.

The door to their room slammed shut, which meant Noah had left.

She slid her body to one side and curled up on the floor. Naked. Cold. Alone. Again.

Her worst fears had come to fruition. And it was all her fault.

Again.

~

Noah had stared at the door for a long time. He could hear her crying. He couldn't bring himself to react, or care.

Fourteen years. Fourteen fucking years.

His chest was rising and falling with every deep breath as he reached down to grab a discarded pair of shorts from the floor and then stood to tug them on.

Fuck. Fuck fuck fuck.

Why? Why the hell would she keep something like that from him?

Why didn't she trust him enough to talk to him?

He paced the room, running a hand through his hair. *Dammit.*

They'd had plans together. She knew he'd wanted kids. How could she take off with his child, *his child*, and not even tell him?

How many times had they discussed their future together? It always included kids. *Several* kids. *Fuck.*

He made his way to the open sliding door and gripped the frame, staring at nothing. He couldn't think. A ringing noise had started in his ears the moment she told him she'd been pregnant. And then she'd rambled on about the reasons *she'd* determined it was necessary to leave him. Sobbing, gasping words about how a child would have messed up their plans. *His* plans.

Why?

Slowly he inhaled, letting his eyes close, as he finally began to understand what she'd said just moments ago. Navy, SEALs, marriage, kids… In that order. She'd known he wouldn't do the first two if pregnancy had forced them to skip to steps three and four.

She was right.

She was also wrong. Wrong to take that choice from him.

He couldn't breathe. He needed to get out of that tiny cabin. So, he spun around and headed for the door.

It took Ellie more than an hour to pull herself off the floor and reach for the shower. She turned it on and crawled inside, not caring that the water was freezing cold. She huddled in the corner for a while on her ass with her knees to her chest again, and when the water got warm enough, she let it run over her, not bothering with soap or shampoo or anything.

When she started to shudder under the spray, she turned it off and somehow managed to pull to standing, grab a towel, and wrap it around her.

A glance in the mirror showed a woman she didn't know. Her eyes were swollen and bloodshot. Her face was red and splotchy. Her hair was plastered to her head. She didn't care. She didn't even bother to dry off. She needed to climb back into the bed before she fainted.

When she twisted the knob and opened the door,

she jumped back so hard she hit her hip on the sink. A small shriek escaped her lips.

Noah was sitting on the edge of the bed, inches from her. His gaze was on hers. Intense. She couldn't begin to read it. But what was he doing there? He was wearing a pair of shorts now. Nothing else. His hair was a mess from running his fingers through it.

"You left," she pointed out.

He sighed. "Apparently not."

"But I heard you leave."

"I wanted to. I tried to. But I couldn't do it." He reached out a trembling hand and grabbed her wrist, drawing her from the bathroom. He scooted to one side, pulled her next to him, and then wrapped an arm around her shoulders.

She had no idea what to make of his reaction, so she sat stiffly, wishing he had left so she could mourn in peace.

Suddenly, he dipped down, tucked a hand under her knees, and lifted her into the air.

She gasped as he settled her in the middle of the bed, climbed up behind her, pulled the covers over them, and then held her trembling body with both arms wrapped tightly around her.

Tears that shouldn't have had enough moisture to form fell again down her cheeks. "Let me go, Noah," she croaked out. "I need to be alone."

"Never," he murmured in her ear. "Never again."

She cried harder, her body shaking. She didn't deserve this kindness.

He held her while she cried, eventually stroking her

skin, brushing her damp hair from her face. She was shivering from being wet and cold. He did his best to stave off the violent shaking.

"I don't deserve this. Please let me go, Noah," she finally pleaded again. "You should be extremely pissed right now."

"I am, but I'll get over it."

She stiffened. Get over it? How was that possible? She hadn't gotten over it in fourteen years. "I treated you horribly. I shouldn't have left you. I didn't know what to do. I made a rash decision. It was wrong of me."

"You must have been so scared," he soothed. "I can't imagine what that was like for you. I'm so sorry I wasn't there for you."

She twisted her face to glance at him. "What are you talking about? I broke up with you. It's my fault."

He shrugged. "I knew something was terribly wrong. I have to take some of the blame. I could have gone after you. Eventually I would have found you. Instead, I let my ego get in the way. I told myself if you wanted to break up with me, fine. I wouldn't stop you."

"It wasn't your choice."

"Of course it was." He gave her a wry smile. "You were mine. Mine to protect and cherish and hold. I know we weren't engaged yet, but we were in love. I knew early in our relationship that you were the one for me. There had never been a doubt."

"And then I dumped you."

He sighed. "But I knew you well enough to know it made no sense. You would never dump me. The about-face was too jarring. If I hadn't been so hurt and angry, I would have realized it made no sense even with your excuses."

"I didn't want to ruin your plans."

"I know, baby." He cupped her face. "I know. I see that now. It's going to take me some time to absorb it all, but bear with me while I process. I've only had an hour. You've had years."

She lowered her head back to the bed, no longer facing him, also processing this weird, unexpected twist.

"Where did you go?" he asked. He had a right to know everything now.

"To the cabins where my parents used to take me when I was a kid. I knew I could afford one for a while."

He kept stroking her skin. "How many people knew?"

"No one. I didn't tell anyone. When it was over, I went back to my parents' house for the summer and then left for college. They knew something had happened to me. So did Karla. But I hid in my room and shut them all out. I'm sure I scared them, but I was adamant about never talking about why we broke up. I was crazed. And then I was numb."

He paused, and then he kissed her shoulder. She was certain she felt tears on his cheek as he leaned against her. His voice was rough when he continued. "Did you see a doctor?"

"No. I took five of those tests. I knew. I didn't need a doctor."

"How did you afford the medical care when you miscarried? Who took you to the hospital?"

She sucked in a breath and twisted her face deeper into the pillow. Renewed sobs wracked her body. The most pain she'd ever felt dragged to the surface.

"Baby…" He was in her space, leaning over her, pulling her so that she couldn't hide from him any longer. He deserved the details. It was just so hard to tell them.

"I never went to the doctor." She hiccupped. "I stayed in that cabin for two weeks, scared out of my mind. I couldn't eat because I was too depressed, and what I did eat, I vomited. I'm sure it was my fault the baby died. I wasn't taking care of myself. I couldn't keep food down. I cried all the time. I figured I was about eleven weeks when it happened."

He held her tighter, tears running down his face.

She forced the rest out. "I woke up to the feeling of warm wetness flowing out of my body. It was the middle of the night. So much blood. I screamed, but no one heard me. The cabin was too isolated. My cries were too weak. I didn't have the strength to move, so I just lay there cramping and shaking all night long while our baby flowed out of me. I knew I was losing a lot of blood, but I didn't care if I died."

"Jesus, Ellie." He cried out loud now, holding her and rocking her and crying openly. "I'm so sorry, baby."

"I lay there in my bloody mess for twelve hours before I managed to crawl to the bathtub and climb into it. The cramping was so painful. I couldn't believe I was still alive. Somehow I managed to survive. I know now there was no reason I would have died from a miscarriage, but at the time it seemed like I'd bled to death."

He closed his eyes, but didn't let her go. "How long did you stay there?"

"It took me another day to have the strength to stand, and then I finally managed to eat something small. If I hadn't been in the tub where I got plenty of water to drink, I might not be here. I was so weak. I curled up in the armchair and wrapped my jacket around my naked body for the entire first night. The bed was covered in blood, all the blankets ruined."

She sucked in a long breath and finished. "After a few days, my brain kicked into gear, and I managed to clean up the mess, stuff the ruined linens in a trash bag, and haul everything to the dumpster. I waited another few days before I returned home."

"Your parents *never* knew?"

"No. When I got home, they knew I'd broken up with you because the entire town knew. I told them I had gone to the cabin to think and that I didn't want to ever discuss it. They probably didn't question my weight loss or how weak I was because they figured it was from mourning our breakup."

"That would make sense." He wiped a tear from his face. "You are so strong and so brave. How did I get so lucky as to have the privilege of finding you again?"

She pursed her lips and closed her eyes.

"I know you feel confused and horrified and so many other emotions they're impossible to put words to right now, but we're going to get through this. I promise you." He laid his head down behind her, still stroking her skin.

She fell asleep in his arms and slept fitfully. Every time she jerked awake, he was still there, holding her, soothing her. He even tucked one leg over hers. Enveloping her completely.

He loved her that much.

CHAPTER 14

Noah stared at his sweet, precious Ellie for hours while she slept. The sun rose higher in the sky while he held her. He was a mix of emotions himself, but he went over everything a hundred times.

It would take days, weeks, maybe months to fully process everything. He would have more questions. He needed to know every detail. He wanted to feel like he'd been there with her.

His guilt wasn't entirely rational, but he meant it when he said he was also to blame for letting her walk away from him. How many times had he painted their future all wrapped up in a tidy package with a perfect bow on top? He could imagine what she might have been thinking when she found out she was pregnant. Things weren't going according to plan. They were so young.

He would have dropped everything for her, and

she'd known that. And it had contributed to her decisions.

Yes, he'd been shocked and then incredibly angry when she first told him about the pregnancy, but then he'd come slowly to his senses. He wasn't completely innocent in the unfolding saga. By the time she'd opened that bathroom door, broken and defeated, he'd been ready to catch her.

And Ellie deserved to be caught. She had gone through all of that pain—physical and emotional— alone. She could have died. He could have lost her because he was too pigheaded to chase her down.

He couldn't imagine how horrifying it must have been for her to miscarry alone in that cabin. Bleeding. The loss of their baby bearing down on her like a lead weight.

Ellie stirred several times, a nightmare grasping her in its clutches. He never let her go. Each time he kissed her temple and whispered words she couldn't hear.

Finally, she opened her eyes and slowly blinked at him.

His arm was asleep under her head, but he didn't care. In the depths of her eyes, he saw a glimpse of the woman he'd fallen in love with and would convince to take him into her life again.

"I'm so sorry," she murmured.

"I know, baby. Me too. But it's over now. And we're going to learn to move forward. Together this time." He clasped her head. "You'll never go through anything like that alone again."

"You can't stay with me, Noah. I'm broken."

He chuckled. "You're just a little chipped. We'll smooth the edges and heal the hurt."

She shook her head, worrying him now. "No. You don't understand. I'm…" She took a breath. "I can't sleep with you. I mean, I can't have sex with you."

"Why not?" Had she suffered some kind of damage? That didn't seem likely. He'd fingered her twice. He would have noticed if she'd had scarring or something. People had sex after miscarriages. Besides, if she'd had something to hide, she wouldn't have let him near her tight warmth.

"Because it scares the hell out of me, Noah. I never want to experience something like that again."

"Baby, people have miscarriages. Lots of women have at least one. It's part of life."

She shook her head. "Not like that. Not so violently."

"Then we won't have kids. If that's what you want." The idea made his chest tighten, but he'd do it for her if she was really that scared.

Her eyes widened. "We weren't having kids that time either, Noah. We used protection. It went wrong. It can always go wrong." Her words trailed off, and she tipped her head down so he couldn't see her expression.

"So let me get this straight. You haven't had sex with anyone for fourteen years because you were afraid you might get pregnant?" He tried to get her to look at him, but she didn't budge.

"Basically. That and…"

"And what?" His confusion mounted.

"And they weren't you."

A smile spread across his face, and he blew out the

longest, most relieved breath of his life. He was a pig for finding that endearing, but he couldn't help it. "Well, I'm here now. And I'm definitely *me*. So, I think it's time you consider how irrational that fear is and toss it overboard. Now's a good time since we're on a ship."

She lay quiet for a long time, and he prayed to God he'd gotten through to her. It made his chest swell that she'd saved herself for him, but then again, that wasn't what happened at all. She'd closed herself off from all men, including him.

Nevertheless, no matter how he sliced it, this precious woman he loved more than anything in the world had only had sex with him. And he was about to convince her she could do so again. And then he was going to convince her to marry him first chance they got. And then they were going to move in together and build a life. He figured he could surely talk her into a few kids if he nurtured her and got her some help and remained patient.

First, he needed to point out that she was a sexual being with a warped fear that she could overcome. He'd never seen anyone so vulnerable and expressive when they orgasmed. Maybe she would only respond that forcefully with *him* because she felt so deeply for him. They would never know because there wasn't a snowball's chance in hell she was ever going to find herself in another man's arms, let alone his bed.

His chest swelled again. He needed to rein it in before he got a complex. Suddenly, he had an idea. He jumped to his knees, straddled her body, and pinned her to the bed on her back.

Her eyes were wide with the shock. The sheet fell away from her breasts, and she was in a tangle of towel and blankets, but he didn't care. The knotted mess might work out in his favor if she tried to escape after he said what he was going to say next.

"What are you doing?" she asked, eyes wild.

"Marry me."

She flinched. Her hands went to the sheets at her waist and tugged.

He grabbed her wrists and pinned them above her head. "Marry me."

She shook her head. "That's crazy. I just told you I wouldn't even sleep with you, and now you want to marry me?"

"Yep. Now. Today. Before we get off this ship."

"You've lost your mind. Is that even a thing?"

He shrugged. "I have no idea. We'll find out. Say yes."

She drew her eyes together. "That's absurd."

He shook his head. "Nope. It's the most rational thought I've had all week. Marry me."

"Did you miss the part about me not having sex with you?"

He rolled his eyes. "You are so totally having sex with me today. If it bothers you, we can do it now and get it over with. Or we can wait until after you've said *I do*, and I've stuck a ring on your finger."

Laughter bubbled out of her throat. Not what he'd had in mind.

"Ellie, I'm totally serious."

"You're totally out of your head. We don't even know each other that well."

"That's bullshit. Try again."

"We don't live in the same state."

"Also a piss-poor argument since technically I don't live in any state and can go wherever I want. And you just quit your job, so you too are free to make changes. If you want to live in New York, we'll live in New York. If you want to move somewhere else, we'll make that happen."

She rolled her eyes. "You have such a tidy answer for everything."

"Yes. You have more concerns? Throw them at me."

"Noah, you can't marry a woman you haven't had sex with."

"I've had sex with you lots of times, so nice try."

She groaned.

He grinned, knowing he was wearing her down. If he wasn't so totally confident she was head over heels in love with him and always had been, he wouldn't pressure her.

They weren't teenagers anymore. They were grown adults, committing to a life together here and now. They weren't planning a distant future laid out irresponsibly in some randomly selected order through eighteen-year-old eyes. He wanted to marry her *now*. Today. There would be no tidy future plan. The pieces would fall into place. They would roll with whatever the universe handed them and be content that they had each other.

He knew her well. She wanted this as badly as he did. She just needed convincing. "What's the matter? You run out of excuses."

"I need food."

He chuckled, reached across her body, grabbed the phone, and held it to his ear.

"What are you doing?" She looked worried.

A man answered. "Room service. Can I help you?"

He glanced at the clock, saw that it was just after noon, and spoke, "I'd like to order two cheeseburgers with fries."

"Certainly, sir. We'll bring that to your room right away."

"Thank you." He hung up the phone, returned his gaze to a stunned Ellie with huge eyes and an open mouth. "What else you got? Bring it on."

Her face slowly softened until a small smile spread, and then she started giggling. Her giggles changed to full-on laughter that couldn't be contained. She squirmed beneath him to free herself, which he permitted under the circumstances.

Her sexy naked body slid from the bed, and she reached into a drawer to pull out a pair of panties.

He watched her step into them and put them up, and then he wrapped an arm around her middle, leaned over, and snagged a thin white tank top. He handed it to her.

She glared at him.

He stepped between her and the drawers and gave her a gentle shove so she fell back to sitting on the bed. After taking the tank top out of her hand, he pulled it over her head. She at least lifted her arms to let him get it on straight.

"What are you doing, Noah?"

"That's it. That's all you get. You're covered."

She rolled her eyes.

He grinned and leaned down to kiss her. She looked fucking hot in the white lacey bikini panties and the tight tank that hugged her tits perfectly. When he released her lips, he grabbed her waist and hauled her backward until she rested against the headboard.

She was fighting a smile.

There was a God.

He tossed the sheet over her legs so she would be halfway decent when he opened the door, and then he straddled her thighs and rested his butt on her knees, capturing her attention. "Do you want to wear one of the dresses you brought, or do you trust me to shop at the boutiques on the main level and buy you something?"

"For what?" She groaned as she caught his meaning. "Noah…"

"The word I'm looking for is *yes*."

"The word you're looking for is *looney*."

He shrugged. "I'm okay with being a little looney. But you're still going to marry me today."

She chewed on her bottom lip, but she was fighting hard not to giggle. A smile lifted the corners of her mouth. "Karla and Layton would have a field day with this."

He smiled. "They will. Yes. Knowing Karla, she'll be pissed that she didn't get to attend the wedding. But it's all her fault, so she can be disappointed."

"We can't get married today, Noah. You've lost your mind," she repeated.

"My mind is fine. Say *yes*."

She shook her head. "Not a chance."

He slid his hands up to her waist and tickled her.

She buckled forward, batting at his hands, laughing so hard it was refreshing after the rough, emotional morning they'd had. "Stop it," she gasped, squirming under him even though he outweighed her by so much she would never succeed in escaping.

"Marry me. Say yes." He stopped tickling her, held her waist, and stared into her eyes.

She wiggled beneath him, her sweet thighs making his cock jump to attention. She glanced down at his predicament and then slid her small hands to cup him. "We haven't had sex, Noah."

"We can fix that." His voice was deeper, husky, hopeful.

She met his gaze. "I'm scared."

"I know. But I'll be with you."

She smiled. "I should hope so."

"You're mine, baby. All I care about is ensuring you understand that we're never separating from each other again. When we get off this ship tomorrow, we aren't going our separate ways. Not even for a moment. We can go visit your parents for a few days and then mine and stop somewhere in that path to kill our friends or thank them…"

"You're rambling." Her smile was growing.

He leaned closer. "Say *yes*."

"We don't have to get married just to stay together."

"Oh, that's not why we're getting married. We're getting married because we should have done so fourteen years ago. We're getting married because we love each other and we want to spend the rest of our lives together."

She nodded slightly, though he wasn't sure which part she was agreeing with. The fact that they should have done so already or the fact that they loved each other. He'd take either.

"I love you," he whispered.

Smile.

"I love you," he repeated.

"I love you too. You know I do." Her voice was soft.

"Then marry me."

She giggled.

A knock sounded at the door, and Noah jumped off her to retrieve their burgers. He took the tray, thanked the guy, and turned back around to find Ellie with the sheet pulled up her body. Good.

"I'm starving," she admitted, dropping the sheet and curling her legs up under her. "Set that right here." She pointed at the bed in front of her. "What are you going to eat?" she joked as she picked up one of the two burgers.

He snagged the other and settled on the edge of the bed. "This is just an appetizer. I didn't think either of us would have the energy to get dressed to go in search of food. After we're rejuvenated from this snack, we can go eat one of everything on the ship."

She moaned around her bite and grabbed a fry. "How did I get this hungry?"

"Stress."

"Yeah." She stuffed more fries in her mouth.

He loved that she didn't care about eating savagely in front of him.

He leaned over and wiped catsup from the corner of her mouth with a napkin.

She came back to life with each bite. She'd needed fuel more than anything after the morning they'd had.

They scarfed everything down in relative silence, and then he cleared the bed, set the tray on the desk, and climbed back over her. "Yes?"

"You're relentless."

"Not going to stop until you say *yes*."

"What if I agree to marry you, but it's not today?"

He shook his head. "It has to be today."

"Why?" She furrowed her brow.

"Because I don't want to wait another day or week or month. I want you to be mine now. You can't escape me as easily if I slap a ring on you and you've signed the papers.

"I know you. You'll come up with ten excuses tomorrow and put it off. Your mom will decide we need a big wedding and convince us to wait a year. Karla will pitch a fit and want to get involved. You'll worry about your job and your hair and your dress and your apartment."

She lifted a hand, palm out. "Okay. I get it. You're right. Especially the part about my mom. The thought of planning a big wedding makes my stomach churn."

He grinned. "See? It would be so much easier to show up and announce it's a done deal. Flash the ring. Show everyone the license. Accept their hugs and congratulations. Done."

"What ring? We don't have a ring?"

"Ellie, there are ten jewelry stores on this ship that would love to sell me a ring today. Do you know how many people get engaged on cruise ships?"

"Ha." She pointed at him. "Engaged. Not married."

He reached down, gave her waist a jerk so she fell onto her back, and smoothed his hand up her body until he was cupping her breast.

She sucked in a sharp breath. "Noah…"

He flicked his thumb over her nipple, hoping to get her pliant enough to stop coming up with excuses. It might have been a cheating move, but the way her face softened told him he was winning.

"You can't ply me with sex, Noah," she said as she reached up to cup his face, her eyes glassy with lust, her lips parted.

He lifted a brow. "No?" He pinched her nipple lightly through the thin white tank. He could see the darkened tip through the material.

She moaned and rolled her head back.

"You're so responsive to me, baby. Your body lights up when I touch you. You're wet, aren't you?"

She squeezed her thighs together under his gaze and bit into her bottom lip.

"Do you love me?" he asked.

"You know I do."

"Say it."

"I have."

"Say it again." He gently twisted that nipple back and forth.

She met his gaze again. "I love you so much it hurts."

173

"Then marry me."

"Okay, but on one condition."

"Anything." His heart pounded.

"Have sex with me first. I need to know."

Breath whooshed from his lungs, and he dipped his face to capture her lips. He'd never been happier.

CHAPTER 15

Ellie thought she was losing her mind as she pulled him closer, easing her hands around to his back. She wanted him more than she'd ever wanted anything in her life. Now.

Noah lifted one knee and planted it between her legs. When his hand slid down to cup her pussy, she parted her legs even farther for him.

She could feel the heat and wetness against his palm. She shuddered, lifting her hips off the bed. A sudden urgency took over. After six days of fighting him off, she wanted him inside her immediately.

She was on fire. Burning from the inside out. Her hands trembled as she reached for the button on his shorts.

He jumped off the bed and shrugged out of them so fast her head was spinning. As soon as he was naked, he bent over, rustled through a bag near the bed, and returned holding a foil packet between two fingers. And then he was there, over her again, jerking her shirt off and then dragging her panties down.

She reached for his hand. "Give me the condom. I want to put it on you."

He handed it to her.

She tore it open and pulled it out. She'd done this before. Not as many times as him, but enough to know how it worked. She also knew there were no guarantees. She rolled it down his length, loving the power and thickness. The heat.

He cupped her face, forcing her to lift her gaze from his erection to his eyes. "It breaks, we deal with it."

She nodded. He was right.

"Together."

She nodded again. She shouldn't be concerned. He loved her. If she got pregnant, he'd be right by her side. If she miscarried, he would hold her hand. If they had a baby, he would *squeeze* her hand. Her fear for the last fourteen years had been irrational.

On the flip side, she might have also leaned on that fear as an excuse, when really she simply didn't want to sleep with anyone else. Anyone who was not Noah.

"How many of those do you have?" she asked.

A slow grin spread. "If we run out, they sell them on the ship, probably in the same store as the diamonds."

"Ha ha."

He sat upright and stared down at her, dancing the tips of his fingers across her breasts, her nipples, her abs, and then lower to tease the sensitive skin of her inner thighs.

"Noah…"

He parted her lower lips, dragged a finger through her folds. Wetness coated his finger, and he lifted it to his mouth to suck it clean. It was the most erotic thing she'd ever seen.

When he set that finger on her clit next and circled it, she grabbed his biceps and lifted her hips. "Okay. Enough foreplay."

"You can never have too much foreplay," he teased.

"'Kay. Save it for later."

He laughed, his finger still working her clit.

"What's so funny?" she whispered, her attention on that finger and its contact point.

"I spent the entire week trying to woo you to open up to me, and now you want fast and furious."

"Yeah. Save slow for later. After…" Her breath hitched. She was struggling to think straight.

"After what, baby?" he whispered as he leaned closer to her so that only an inch separated their lips.

"After we get married," she murmured before realizing what he'd conned her into saying.

His grin was huge and infectious. "Now you're talking."

She dug her fingers into his arms. "Noah. Now."

He released her clit, lined his cock up with her entrance, and thrust home.

She sucked in a sharp breath, her body reacting like a virgin. He was thick. It was tight. She drew in breath, waiting for the burn to dissipate.

When she met his gaze, she found him staring at her intently. His elbows were planted next to her head. His lips were tucked into his teeth.

Slowly, her body accepted the intrusion, and she was left with ten thousand nerve endings that were demanding friction. She licked her dry lips. "Noah, move."

"You okay?" he asked, his thumbs stroking her temples.

"I will be after you make me come."

He smiled again, planted his lips on hers, and pulled partially out.

She groaned around the intensity of the sensations. She had forgotten how good it felt to have him inside her. Foreplay was nice. Any orgasm was always pleasant. He could do amazing things with his mouth and his fingers, but his cock... Damn.

Her vision swam as he thrust harder and faster. Deeper even. He kept his lips on hers, but he must have lost the ability to concentrate on the kiss because they remained parted but no longer moving.

She loved that she did that to him. Made him lose his senses enough that he couldn't focus on anything but his erection and how to best use it in her. And he was a master at driving her to the edge with nothing but his thrusts.

There was no doubt he was larger than he'd been when they were eighteen, but he was also more skilled. She wouldn't even bother concerning herself with thoughts of how he'd developed these skills because from now on, they would be dedicated solely to her benefit.

So good.

She lifted her hips into his thrusts, gasping when the base of his cock hit her clit over and over.

His eyes blinked open, and he met her watery gaze. "God, I love you."

"Love you too," she whispered against his lips. She was so close. She sucked in a breath, dug her nails into his arms, and concentrated on every thrust as it made contact with her clit. So close...

"Come for me, baby."

Those words. The command.

She tipped over the edge just as he sped up his thrusts and followed right behind her. Still thrusting, he made her orgasm drag out forever. She wouldn't mind if he never stopped, but he gradually slowed down until he rested inside her. His hand came to her face, cupping the entire right side. "Marry me."

"Yes."

~

Ellie was a ball of nerves.

She'd spent the last two hours showering and pampering herself. Fixing her hair. Getting her makeup just right. Freaking out.

Her hands shook so badly most of that time that she was afraid she'd get mascara in her eyes.

Noah spent most of that time coming and going from the room. He insisted he needed ten minutes to shower and shave, so he would take care of everything else.

Somehow he'd found out that the ship indeed

performed weddings and would be happy to do so at six o'clock. Most people tended to get married on the first or second night of the cruise, not the last.

She jumped in place as she realized he was behind her again, leaning on the frame of the door. He hadn't stopped smiling since they'd had sex, and she'd said *yes*. "You got everything done?" she asked.

"Yep. And then some. All I need is a shower, and we'll be good to go."

She glanced down at herself. She was wearing a white lace bra and panties, but nothing else. "I might need more clothes."

He kissed her lips. When she started to pass him, he cupped her biceps and held her gaze. "I love you."

"You've mentioned that." Her face hurt from smiling. Ironic since she'd spent the morning crying harder than she'd ever cried in her life. Now she was the happiest woman on earth.

"I bought you a dress. It's hanging in the closet."

"I'll put it on while you shower."

He lifted a hand and stroked her cheek with his thumb. "You're going to marry me."

"Yes." She reached for his T-shirt and fisted it in her hand at his chest. "I am." It seemed like he needed the confirmation, like maybe he feared she would disappear while he was in the shower. "Get moving. We'll be late."

He was still staring at her with a lopsided grin when she shut the door in his face.

She turned around and opened the closet. And then she gasped. "Holy shit." She reached out and fingered the delicate white lace of the bodice, her gaze roaming up and down the most gorgeous dress she'd ever seen.

Most women would have been nervous to let their fiancé choose and purchase a dress for them. But she hadn't worried a moment. She'd known he would pick something perfect. He'd outdone himself.

She was giddy as she slid it off the hanger and held it up against her, spinning around to face the mirror on the inside of the closet door. She immediately knew the upper body was going to fit snug against her breasts and not require a bra, so she removed hers and then stepped into the dress and pulled it into place.

She reached back and tugged the zipper up as far as she could reach, enough to reassure her it was a perfect fit. The fitted silk in front cupped her breasts, lifting them and giving her cleavage.

The edges of the bodice around the swell of her breasts had a row of tiny lace roses, each individually sewn into the silk. It hugged her waist and then flared out, reaching T-length, a layer of tulle underneath giving it some volume. Every few inches there was another row of tiny lace roses.

It was by far the most beautiful thing she'd ever worn. When she took another step back to see herself better, she bumped into a box and glanced down to see it was a shoe box. Inside was a pair of delicate white heels with more roses along the straps.

As she sat on the edge of the bed to fasten them, another surprise caught her eye. A row of tulle lay on the desk. She grinned like a little girl as she rushed over to pick it up. It was a veil, and it was attached to a silver clip for her hair that also had a row of tiny silver roses.

Don't cry, she told herself as she turned toward the mirror and fastened the clip in her hair.

The door opened behind her, and for a moment she stared at Noah's reflection in the mirror. The look on his face made every moment up to this day worth the wait.

He wore a towel on his hips, but he came to her back, finished zipping the dress, and then brushed her hair to one side to kiss her shoulder. "You've never looked more beautiful, baby."

"Thank you." She tipped her head back. "Is that what you're wearing?" she teased.

He winked. "Tonight, on our last night on the ship, I think it's only fitting that *you* wait on the balcony for *me* to get dressed."

She giggled and did as he requested, stepping outside, tipping her head back, and closing her eyes. The peaceful moment alone with the cool breeze on her face was welcome. It helped her center herself.

I'm getting married. To the love of my life. Now. Tonight.

Hands landed on her waist. Lips on her shoulder. The hands slid up to her neck and something cold touched her skin. She glanced down to see him fastening the necklace he'd given her last night. It was perfect. He was perfect.

When she turned around, her breath got caught in her lungs.

He was wearing a black tux with a white shirt and a white bowtie. "You clean up nice," she stated, setting her hands on his shoulders and lifting onto her tiptoes to kiss him. "You're the most handsome man I've ever seen," she added.

He slid his hand into hers and pulled her into the room.

Surprising her, he turned around, clasped both her hands, and lowered to one knee before her.

She fought hard not to cry.

He reached into his pocket and pulled out a small white box, opening it for her to see. Inside was the most beautiful diamond solitaire set in white gold. "Ellington Gorman, will you marry me?"

"Yes." The word was barely audible, but he must have heard her well enough because he picked up the ring, set the box on the bed, and slid it onto her finger. It was an exact fit. Of course.

When he stood, he cupped her face and kissed her gently on the lips. "Let's make you mine."

Holding her hand, he led them from the room.

All along the corridor and then the glass elevator people did a double take and smiled. Without the veil, it might not have been as obvious. The dress was amazing, but it didn't have to be a wedding dress; the length of tulle down her back gave her away.

She blushed repeatedly, her excitement rising at the looks on the faces of perfect strangers. Some of them she recognized from spending a week on the ship, but she didn't know their names or anything about them. And yet, they were all playing a small role to make her day better.

She stepped into a little chapel with Noah at her

side, and it seemed like the next half hour moved in fast motion. A chaplain greeted them, said a few kind words, and invited them to repeat the standard wedding vows she'd heard many times in her life but never had the opportunity to speak herself.

Before she knew it, Noah was holding out a thin white gold band that matched the ring he'd given her less than an hour ago. She couldn't concentrate on the words he spoke because she was busy watching him slide the ring onto her finger and then studying his face. His expression was all that mattered. So much love.

He set another band in her hand, and she repeated the same words as the chaplain read them.

"And now, by the power vested in me, I pronounce you husband and wife. You may kiss the bride."

Noah grabbed her waist and lifted her off the floor, kissing her deeply. When he broke away, people were clapping and giggling in the hallway outside the alcove that served as a ship chapel.

Noah set his forehead against hers and blew out a long breath. "You sure made me work for that this week." His eyes danced with laughter.

"The best things in life are worth the effort," she responded.

CHAPTER 16

No one was waiting for them when they disembarked the next morning. Noah was grateful. He'd half expected to find Karla and Layton standing at the exit, yearning for details.

The truth was Noah wanted his new wife to himself a while longer. He hadn't told her, but he'd booked that night in the honeymoon suite on the top floor of one of Houston's finest hotels.

"Where do we go first?" she asked as they stepped into the sun, wobbling a bit as they shook off their sea legs. Her brow was furrowed with concern. "You have a plan?"

He pointed at the limo that was parked in the pick-up line, the man next to it holding a sign that said: *Mr. and Mrs. Seager.*

Noah watched Ellie's face light up. "You got us a limo?"

"I did more than that. Come on."

She nearly skipped beside him, and he hated that he had to release her hand so they could maneuver their luggage to the awaiting car. When the driver realized they were his passengers, he rushed forward and took Ellie's bags from her.

He loaded everything in the car and introduced himself, and then he held the back door open so they could climb inside.

Ellie's face was lit up. She looked so young and carefree. He imagined she had probably spent the last several years aging. She deserved a break. He knew she was expecting to find a job immediately and go back to work, but he hoped he could convince her to take some time off. Slow down. Live. Smile. Laugh.

Damn, she looked amazing.

He sat back in his seat, watching her as she smiled. "Come here, Mrs. Seager."

She slid closer, and he grabbed her by the waist and pulled her onto his lap. Her eyes twinkled as she kissed him.

"I could kiss you for the rest of eternity."

She giggled, a sound he loved. A sound she'd made many times in the last twenty-four hours. "I'll let you do that, but if you don't mind, I'd also enjoy it if you'd do some of those other things you did to me last night." She flushed.

He held her closer. "Oh, baby, I intend to do so many things to you in the next twenty-four hours that you'll be too tired to get out of bed tomorrow."

"I guess that means we aren't going straight to my mom and dad's," she joked.

"Nope." He couldn't wait to see her excitement when she stepped into their suite and found out it was not only ten times bigger than the cabin on the ship, but it had its own hot tub inset in the floor.

"Whatever you have planned, I already like it."

"I figure we'll leave our phones off, at least for another day. Let Karla and Layton stew over what might have happened to us. Then we'll face the vultures and let them gloat."

"I love it."

"We'll hit your parents' and mine, but please don't let either of them talk us into spending the night. We'll book a hotel nearby. I just got you back. I'm not done making you scream my name several times a day yet. There's no way in hell I'm sleeping under either of our parents' roofs."

"Agreed."

"Thank God. After we've given them a few days, I say we fly to New York. I want to see the apartment my wife has been living in."

"I'll warn you, it's about the size of that ship cabin. It's in Manhattan, after all."

"Does it have a bed?"

She laughed. "Yes."

"That's all I'll need." He kissed her again.

"I guess we could lock ourselves inside for a few weeks and order takeout."

He groaned. "That's the best idea I've heard yet."

He soaked in her expression. So much love and excitement. Her eyes twinkled. "You know I don't care about the size of your apartment. If you want to stay in New York, we will."

She winced. "No. God, no. I'm so over that scene."

He cocked his head to one side. "I'm still not sure I understand how you ended up detouring so far from teaching. It was all you talked about in high school. You and Karla were going to get your education degrees together and then work at the same school and share supplies." He laughed, remembering all their excited plans.

Ellie's face grew serious. "Honestly, I didn't think I could face other people's kids after I lost our baby. I switched from thinking I would have four of my own to believing I would never have a child. I knew that profession would be too painful. So I picked something totally different that I could bury myself in and hide from life.

"New York was as far away as I could get. There were no reminders of you there. I rarely even went home to visit."

"Ellie…" He set his forehead against hers, his throat clogged with emotion. They would have kids. One way or another. He knew she would eventually decide to fill that craving. If she didn't want to give birth to them, they would adopt. There was no way to go back and change the course of events, but he could make up for lost time.

For now, he needed to shake them out of this somber path he'd led them down. He forced a huge smile. "At some point I'll have to pull my tail between my legs and call a few guys from my SEAL team. We're close. They're going to freak out when they find out I ran into my childhood sweetheart and married her in a week. I can't wait for you to meet them."

She smiled. "I'll be honored." And then her smile switched to a giggle. "Is this wine-drinking habit of yours a SEAL thing? Do they all drink dry red?" she teased.

He rolled his eyes. "No. But every one of us does have a particular taste for different alcohols. Except Trevor. He doesn't drink much alcohol, but he's glued to his coffee. Our particular tastes are kind of a running joke. Several of them even nicknamed me Red."

She laughed. "That's funny, since you don't have red hair. What are all these drinks your friends prefer?"

"Let's see…" He glanced at the ceiling, recalling several of his SEAL team with a smile. "Nikko drinks beer. Connor drinks some weird-ass thing called a Rusty Nail. Gunner prefers a single malt. Chase is a salty dog guy."

"What's a salty dog?" She giggled.

"Some shit with grapefruit juice."

She curled up her nose.

He continued. "Carson prefers sex on the beach."

She laughed harder. "That's very girly."

"Don't I know it. Clay drinks a dirty martini. And Asher drinks bourbon neat."

When he finished the rundown, she was grinning even wider from ear to ear. "They're like brothers to you, aren't they?"

"Yes."

"I can't wait to meet them." Her face turned serious.

"I've never been this happy, Noah. Thank you for forcing me to see the truth. I think so much time went by that my view of what happened got warped."

"You own that past, baby. I will never blame you for what happened. In fact, I accept my half of the blame. It's done. It's over. We'll both learn to leave it in the past as we make a life together. I'm not suggesting you bury it yet. I know you'll still need to talk it out some more. You carried a lot of baggage around alone for fourteen years. I will listen to every single word you have to say about it. Always. But at the same time, we're stepping into the future with a clean slate."

A tear slid from her eye, but she wiped it away quickly and nodded. "I can do that."

"*We* can do that. We're doing it together."

For a long time, they stared at each other in silence, the only sound that of the limo as it cruised down the highway.

He searched her face and found nothing but love.

Suddenly she said the most unexpected thing. "My initials are tattooed on your ass."

"Yep. Imagine how I would have explained that to another woman."

She swatted at him playfully. "There was never going to be another woman."

He cupped her face. "That's right. You were always the only woman for me. And as much shit as I'm going to give Layton for meddling in my life, I will forever be grateful for his intervention because I have you back."

"Always." She slid her eyes closed as he took her

mouth, moaning against his lips in that way that made his cock jump to attention.

Thank God it was only another half hour to the hotel. He needed her again. He would need her like a drug for a very long time.

After all, he had years to make up. And she was finally his.

AUTHOR'S NOTE

I hope you enjoyed *Hot SEAL, Red Wine* from the SEALs in Paradise series. Here is a list of the other books in this series:

Hot SEAL, Salty Dog by Elle James
Hot SEAL, S*x on the Beach by Delilah Devlin
Hot SEAL, Dirty Martini by Cat Johnson
Hot SEAL, Bourbon Neat by Parker Kincade
Hot SEAL, Cold Beer by Cynthia D'Alba
Hot SEAL, Rusty Nail by Teresa Reasor
Hot SEAL, Black Coffee by Cynthia D'Alba
Hot SEAL, Single Malt by Kris Michaels

Please enjoy the following excerpt for book one in my Project DEEP series, *Reviving Emily.*

REVIVING EMILY

PROJECT DEEP (BOOK ONE)

Ryan stared at his patient without moving. He'd done so a lot lately. Nearly every waking hour. He couldn't bring himself to leave her side. He told himself it was because she was the most interesting research subject of his career, but he knew he was partially lying.

She was stunning. Even in a hospital bed with no real shower for ten years, limp hair, and pale features, she was gorgeous. Her smile lit up a room. It was irrational for him to be attracted to her, but if he were honest, he'd already held a torch for her from years of studying her research notes. He understood how her brain worked—so much like his it had always sparked an interest. Seeing her… It was like meeting someone he'd known online for years.

He probably needed more sleep. And perhaps he should have taken more time to date in the last decade. It had never seemed as important as his research, however. His parents were preserved in this bunker. He never once felt like he had the right to be out partying and enjoying himself while they were stuck in the underground facility, waiting for a cure.

He *still* didn't have that luxury. His focus needed to be on his parents, reanimating them, and bringing them back to health. A woman had never distracted him from this task before. Why now?

He kept telling himself his attraction had less to do with Emily herself and more to do with the fact that he hadn't dated in a long time, she was stunning, her brain was amazing, and he was so fascinated by her case. Several factors could explain why he was so drawn to her. Combined, they made perfect sense.

If he managed to bring his parents back to life, they would reprimand him for not living life, but it couldn't be helped. The few times in college he'd allowed someone to lure him out to a bar or a party had left him feeling restless, guilt climbing up his spine.

So, no. He had not lived life as his parents had instructed. He had dedicated himself to finding a cure and gathering other scientists to help him. The task had been monumental. For one thing, there had been a constant need to acquire funding.

Luckily, the government had made a particular arrangement with every member of the original team to pay out what essentially amounted to death benefits to their families. The benefits would be paid for as long as the twenty-two people were in a state of suspension. The benefits would end when and if the people were able to return to their regular lives, or, in the event of their deaths, the benefits would switch to a lump sum to be paid out to the families.

For Ryan, the money was enough to live off of. It covered his tuition, and it provided him with the means to begin researching on his own after graduating at the top of his class in med school. Luckily, he always had his grandmother to fall back on. She still lived in his childhood home. The two of them were close, and Ryan always knew he had somewhere to get away and someone who cared about him.

For the first year after residency, he'd worked alone, often from the small bedroom in his childhood home. He spent half his time with his head buried in research and the other half pleading with the government to reopen the study and fund him. Eventually, they had acquiesced, giving him three people for the first six months and then gradually increasing his team until they numbered a dozen in total.

He had no illusion that the reason the government let him form a team initially had nothing to do with the twenty-two suspended souls. The reason they'd permitted him to continue the research where his parents had left off was because a cure still needed to be developed before AP12 took hundreds of thousands of lives.

It wasn't simply the disease that needed to be cured, though. He simultaneously needed cryonicists working on a way to reanimate the team. The cure itself would be useless to the team if there was no way to bring the preserved people back to life.

When Ryan discovered Dr. Damon Bardsley

working in a research facility in the fields of cryobiology and cryonics, he'd approached him and brought him on board. The two of them were the only two people on the team who weren't military. The only two civilians who had any knowledge of the project and its possibilities. The other ten members were all military, as were all twenty-two of the people who had been preserved.

A soft sigh jerked his attention back to the woman lying on the bed as she blinked her eyes open and then smiled. "Is it real? Or am I having a dream? I keep waking up to find you leaning over me. If I'm dead, this is certainly what I would have wanted heaven to be like."

He blinked, speechless. What had she implied?

Her smile broadened. "You heard me. You're not hard on the eyes."

He chuckled, but he did it while brushing a lock of hair from her face and then continuing to stroke her cheek with his thumb. He was drawn to her like a magnet, unable to stop himself from touching her. "Well, Emily Zorich, if we're having a confessional, you're not hard on the eyes either." Some alien being had possessed his body. Since when did he flirt with women?

She rolled those eyes at his statement. "I haven't seen a mirror yet, but I also haven't had a shower in ten years. Nor have I had a comb or makeup or a toothbrush or a manicure."

He glanced toward her hand, lifted it, and held it in

front of his face. "Did you get a lot of manicures back then?"

She giggled, the sweetest sound. "I've never actually had one. It just sounded like something I should list." She narrowed her gaze. "Did I know you? It doesn't seem possible. Obviously you weren't working here ten years ago. You can't be more than about twenty-five. And I so rarely left the bunker. You must just look familiar."

He gave her hand a squeeze. "I'm thirty, technically a year older than you. I don't remember meeting you, but it's possible you saw me or even interacted with me at some point when I was in my teens. My parents are Tushar Anand and Trish Wolbach-Anand."

The Art of Kink:

Pose

Paint

Sculpt

Arcadian Bears:

Grizzly Mountain

Grizzly Beginning

Grizzly Secret

Grizzly Promise

Grizzly Survival

Grizzly Perfection

Sleeper SEALs:

Saving Zola

Spring Training:

Catching Zia

Catching Lily

Catching Ava

The Underground series:

Force

Clinch

Guard

Submit

Thrust

Torque

Saving Sofia (Kindle World)

Wolf Masters series:

Kara's Wolves

Lindsey's Wolves

Jessica's Wolves

Alyssa's Wolves

Tessa's Wolf

Rebecca's Wolves

Melinda's Wolves

Laurie's Wolves

Amanda's Wolves

Sharon's Wolves

Claiming Her series:

The Rules

The Game

The Prize

Emergence series:

Bound to be Taken

Bound to be Tamed

Bound to be Tested

Bound to be Tempted

The Fight Club series:

Come

Perv

Need

Hers

Want

Lust

Wolf Gatherings series:

Tarnished

Dominated

Completed

Redeemed

Abandoned

Betrayed

Durham Wolves series:

Rescue in the Smokies

Fire in the Smokies

Freedom in the Smokies

Stand Alone Books:

Blind with Love

Guarding the Truth

Out of the Smoke

Abducting His Mate

ABOUT THE AUTHOR

Becca Jameson is the best-selling author of over 60 books. She is most well-known for her Wolf Masters series and her Fight Club series. She currently lives in Atlanta, Georgia, with her husband, two grown kids, and the various pets that wander through. She is loving this journey and has dabbled in a variety of genres, including paranormal, sports romance, military, and BDSM.

A total night owl, Becca writes late at night, sequestering herself in her office with a glass of red wine and a bar of dark chocolate, her fingers flying across the keyboard as her characters weave their own stories.

During the day--which never starts before ten in the morning!--she can be found jogging, floating in the pool, or reading in her favorite hammock chair!

...where Alphas dominate...

Contact Becca:
Webpage: www.beccajameson.com
Email: beccajameson4@aol.com
Facebook: becca.jameson.18
Twitter: @beccajameson

Made in the USA
Monee, IL
29 July 2022

10540522R00118